Books by Kathleen Pennell

Pony Investigator Series
The Case of the Missing Money
The Case of the Phantom Stallion
The Case of the Midnight Stranger
The Case of the Mysterious Circus
The Case of the Secret Passage
The Case of the Mirror Image

The Adventures In Time Series
The Door into Time
Rescued in Time
Lancelot Maddox Series
The Boy on the Bench
Ragtag Rescue
The Missing Agent
Plane Down

A Treadwell Mystery Series
The Face in the Water
The Man at the Ruins

A Treadwell
Mystery #2

THE MAN AT THE RUINS

Kathleen Pennell

May 1977

Grayson Matthews stood over his wife's bed as blood seeped from her body. Her skin grew pale and her breathing became shallow. When Vera walked through the hospital room door, Grayson's head shot up then his eyes dropped. But it was too late. They both knew what had just taken place and why. Justice would be served but it would take nineteen years and a great deal of planning before it came to fruition.

Chapter 1

April 19, 1996

Three people arrived at the top of the cliff directly above the ruins. The driver parked beside another car but they wouldn't see the fourth person until they reached their destination. The atmosphere was thick with unspoken tension.

The man stared at Job and Hannah as they stood beside his car. He unbuttoned his suit coat, loosened his tie, turned on his heel, and began to walk. He felt a deep, smug satisfaction knowing this little problem would be resolved before a lawsuit deprived him of a lifestyle he'd come to expect.

Hannah, dressed in slacks, polo shirt, and a light jacket, followed one step behind. She glanced over her shoulder at Job who brought up the rear by several yards. He stared at the ground with his hands stuffed inside his jeans pockets. His lips formed a straight, tight line because he'd done his homework and knew the reason for Vera's call. What was in it for the retired nurse? Was it a simple case of justice served or was there something more?

His eyes rose and stared at the back of the young woman who claimed to be his sister. Vera said they shared the same distinguishing characteristic. The distinguishing characteristic was evident. But, with millions of dollars at stake, that swath of blond hair in the front could easily be dyed to deceive him.

They walked one hundred yards to the spot carefully chosen the previous week and stood beside an iron rail fence along the cliff installed years ago to ensure that visitors didn't fall over the edge to their death. Job and Hannah glanced occasionally at each other wondering how long he intended to play this vicious game of cat and mouse and how it would end. With each glance, they took measure of each other unsure where the other's loyalties lay.

Job and Hannah detected a slight movement within the dense brush thirty feet away. But all was quiet when they turned to see what or who it was. With a growing sense of uneasiness, they refocused their attention on the man who stood before them.

He reached inside an inner pocket and withdrew a check. "Do you want to know the amount of this check and whose name is written on it?" he said, barely above a whisper? it was a rhetorical question for which he didn't expect a response, so he wasn't disappointed when none was forthcoming.

The other two kept their eyes focused on his face rather than what he held. They had a very good idea whose name was on it. They were only curious about how much he thought their silence was worth. There wasn't a check large enough to buy their silence.

"Now," he said waving the check in front of them. "I won't take advantage of your youth and inexperience. I have two checks made out. One for each of you. Equal amounts, naturally. The checks will be yours as soon as you sign a little paper. Just a formality, you understand."

Job was tempted to clasp the hand of Hannah in a show of solidarity. But would the tension escalate because the man would detect a unity between them he hadn't predicted. And could he expect unity with this young woman who called herself Hannah? He stood tall, without expression, and without breaking eye contact.

The man extended his hand holding the check. When the two young people refused to accept it, he tore the check into eight tiny pieces and tossed them into the air where a steady breeze carried them over the cliff. He waited a few seconds then withdrew a second check. "Plenty here for both of you. You can divide it and still live rather comfortably." When they refused to accept the second check, his face hardened as he torn it up and disposed of it.

What happened next was done with such lightning speed that it was impossible to give a reliable testimony to the sequence of events.

A struggle ensued. The two were of equal size, equal strength, and determination. One survived while the other fell over the cliff to his death.

Chapter 2

April 5, 1996 – Two Weeks Earlier

Vera made three phone calls that morning which would change the trajectory of several lives. The first call was to a man who referred to himself as Job. He was known by another name but thought of himself as Job for he had suffered much.

When Job answered, she said, "You have a sister."

"What are you talking about?"

"You have a sister," Vera repeated. "She calls herself Hannah."

"You have the wrong number. I don't have a sister named Hannah or any other sister."

"I have the right number, and you do have a sister. I didn't say her name was Hannah. I said she calls herself Hannah."

"She calls herself Hannah," Job said softly. Not a religious person, he knew enough that Job had suffered. He also knew there was a woman named Hannah who had also suffered.

"Who are you?" Job said.

"My name is Vera. I'm a retired nurse."

"What makes you think I have a sister?"

"I was there when she was born," Vera said then added gently. "And I was there when your mother died shortly after that." She paused a moment. "Hannah has a distinguishing characteristic that is identical to yours, so I know she's your sister."

Job's hair was light brown except for a blond, two-inch swath that started at the front and ran several inches towards the back of his head. That distinguishing characteristic hadn't so much as set Job apart as been a curiosity his entire life. "I don't understand any of this."

"I'm sorry. I know this is a shock, but there's a reason I called," Vera said. "Hannah lived in Cameron most of her life. Recently, she moved closer to you. A sweet girl. But like you, an unhappy one."

Job was silent for a moment as he pondered what this woman said. Vera spoke with such assuredness. There were a dozen questions he should have asked but he wouldn't think of them till later. "All right. I have no idea what you're talking about, but I'm prepared to believe you. How can I have a sister that I know nothing about?"

"That story belongs to your father."

"Both my parents are dead."

"No," Vera said. "Your mother died; your father is still alive."

Job cupped his head in his left hand. "No. You're wrong. They died, I arranged their funeral, I sold our house."

"I know all about that, Job," Vera said softly. "I need to make two more phone calls. Trust me, your father is alive."

"But who is this man you claim is my father? If I do have a father, why haven't I heard from him all these years?" Job said.

For the first time, Vera hesitated. "I know why he hasn't contacted you. As far as his identity, I suspect his name will be in the newspaper very shortly. No photo. He's been very careful about that. You'll know why later." Again she hesitated. "I suspect you won't have to look for him. He'll look for you and your sister."

"He'll look for me and my sister?" Job said trying to decide if that was good or bad. "Why won't you tell me who he is now?"

"Because it may not be—in your best interest to contact him. Just be prepared when he does."

"Is he that dangerous?"

"Can be," Vera said. "I should say, he has been."

Suddenly, one question became abundantly clear. "If you were there when Hannah was born and my mother died, why have you waited all these years to call me?"

"You're twenty-one now. You're of legal age. You can fight your father in court for what is rightfully yours and hers if need be. Somehow, I doubt if it comes to that," Vera said. "Be careful. I have to leave now."

Job considered everything she said while a slow anger grew within him.

Vera called a well-remembered number. "Sue Ellen?"

"Where are you?"

"At home. The car is packed and I'm ready to leave but I wanted to see how you are first. And I wanted to know if you're prepared for what's ahead."

"I don't know. I won't know until I'm there," Sue Ellen said in a strained voice.

"I'm going to call someone shortly and I suspect—no, I know that will set off a chain reaction."

"Will it impact me?"

"Yes."

"Then don't call!"

"I'm sorry, Sue Ellen. I'd spare you the fallout if I could. And I wish it were that simple but it's not."

"I have no idea what to expect or how to handle this and I need your help."

"Don't worry, I'll be nearby." Sue Ellen waited while Vera weighed what needed to be said. "A young woman has been hired. She's an impersonator. Quite good at her job. Has done it before."

"An impersonator," Sue Ellen said softly.

"That's where you come in. You need to be the eyes and ears and report to me."

"I'm worried about what might happen," Sue Ellen said.

"The person I'll call next doesn't do the dirty work himself. He uses someone else for that," Vera said. "There were four of us who grew up in the same town, went to the same school. Two boys; two girls. The boys were always fierce competitors. They haven't changed. I've thought carefully about whether or not I should call them. But there's no way to resolve this issue."

"Can't you tell me more about them, what to expect, and where you will be?" Sue Ellen said.

"No, I can't do that. It's important that you know enough to be on your guard. If he sees that you are anticipating what he is about to do, he'll become suspicious. That will be infinitely worse for you." Vera let that sink if before continuing. "I'll stand back without anyone knowing where I am and just let him—hang himself," she said then repeated the same question she had earlier. "How are you?"

"I'm afraid," Sue Ellen whispered.

"I know, so am I--Hannah."

"Yes, I am no longer Sue Ellen. I'm Hannah now."

"Remember Anne," Vera said then disconnected to make her next call.

"Remember Anne," Sue Ellen said softly. On a small piece of paper she wrote those words in upper case letters. "REMEMBER ANNE". Folding the paper, she slipped it inside her billfold. When she grew worried or afraid, she would refer to that paper and it would renew her courage.

Chapter 3

April 5, 1996

After Vera discontinued the call with Sue Ellen, she called the man she hadn't seen for nineteen years. "It's Vera," she said. When the man didn't respond, she added. "You know who I am. I was the nurse who was with your wife when she died." Again there was silence, but this time she waited.

"What do you want?" the man said warily.

"I called your son a few moments ago and told him a few things he has a right to know," Vera said. She patiently waited through another period of silence.

"I don't know what you mean."

"Oh, I think you know exactly what I mean."

Beads of perspiration appeared on his forehead and he loosened his tie. "You're lying," he whispered. "Besides, if you suspected something, you would have—notified someone."

"My word against yours. Shortly after your wife died, I recorded a statement with someone trustworthy and signed it. it's somewhere safe. It was merely a question of waiting until your son was of age." Vera said.

He moistened his lips. "How much do you want?"

"That's so like you to think I want something," Vera said. "Nothing, I want nothing."

"Why now? it must be almost twenty years since her death."

"Nineteen years to be exact. I waited until your son was old enough to legally fight his own battles."

"Is warning me some kind of favor?" he said sarcastically.

"No, you don't deserve any favors," Vera said. "I'm telling you because I'd like to see you squirm for a while before your sins catch up with you."

"What sins?"

"Remember Anne," Vera said.

He kept his temper which was rare for him. Quietly, he said, "Where are you?"

Vera's lips formed a tight smile. "It doesn't matter because I'm going to a place where you can't find me."

"And you think you can get away with this?"

"I'm not the one who has gotten away with something all these years. But the tide has shifted. And I hope the tide takes you right out to sea with it." And with that, she disconnected the call, got in her car, and left town.

He sat for a moment contemplating his next move. Phone calls were made. Discreet questions leveled in measured tones. He studied and memorized the notes he'd taken one last time before he destroyed them. One crucial item stood out. Both his children lived in Bedford. Very convenient. When he'd gathered enough information, he called Leto, who was an expert at cleaning up after him.

Leto recognized the caller and answered with the descriptive nickname he'd assigned to him, "Hey, Diablo. Good to hear from you."

Diablo loathed that name, but Leto never failed to complete an assignment. He had one more quality that was crucial. He kept his mouth shut. "I need you to do something for me, Leto."

"I know, Diablo. Otherwise you wouldn't have called. So what is it this time?" Leto said in a bored voice permitted only by someone who was indispensable.

Diablo sucked in his utter contempt for Leto as he related the history behind the phone call he'd received from Vera. The story went back nearly two decades and was one he'd never revealed to anyone much less to his childhood competitor. He also described what he wanted done. He left the details to Leto.

"Okay." Leto tapped his fingertips on his desk. "It'll take a week perhaps longer to come up with a plan. I'll call you when everything is in place," he said. After the call ended, he sat back and reviewed the facts.

There was a private detective Leto knew who didn't mind getting his hands dirty. What Leto knew, he repeated to the private detective. Job was twenty-one and Hannah was nineteen. They lived in or near Bedford. The detective returned Leto's call three days later revealing the addresses, phone numbers, and places of employment of Job and Hannah.

Before he made the two phone calls, Leto carefully deliberated what he would say to them. His proposal must sound inviting without giving away too much information and without a hint of a threat.

After successfully completing those calls, he drew a diagram of the players and listed the sequence of events that had to take place in the exact order if the plan was to be successful. Would it work? What if he was betrayed. What if… The what ifs consumed him and threatened to derail his plans.

He needed a holding place in the worst-case scenario. The house must be secure and remote. Only someone who was desperate would consider adding the necessary modifications to the house he needed to rent. The person he called vacillated until he upped the ante. After the price was settled, it became a question of how to fulfill the requirements without drawing too much attention to odd requests. Perhaps several workmen would be called in so that no one person was responsible for the entire project. Having settled that, Leto moved on.

Emotions can be dangerous unless channeled in the desired direction. After careful consideration, he contacted a young woman who had worked with him once before. As Diablo foolishly trusted him, he trusted her. They tossed out suggestions that impacted the life, death, and freedom of several people as some might discuss where to have dinner that night. And as they spoke, a spark of greed ignited that would grow in intensity until someone got burned.

Diablo and Leto sat at their desks thinking and plotting. Their goals were diametrically opposed to each other. And by the end of two weeks, only one would survive.

Chapter 4

April 19, 1996, At the top of the cliff

Initially, one man grabbed Hannah's purse while the other manhandled Job's phone from him. Neither Job nor Hannah had anticipated the attack and weren't prepared to defend themselves.

It was horrifying. Each man tried to catapult the other one over the rail to his death below the cliff. Job and Hannah had never witnessed this level of violence before.

The two young people backed up and retraced their steps along the pathway, picking up speed until they were running. Their shocked minds drove them to flee the same way they had arrived. The realization that neither of them had a key to either car came slowly.

They were twenty miles out of town in the middle of nowhere. Rising panic clouded their judgment and they stopped suddenly, unsure how to escape.

The brush and trees to the left weren't thick, but they grew over their heads and would hide them within thirty feet of entry. The struggle and raised voices behind them covered the sound of them crashing through the brush. Their only concern was putting as much distance between themselves and the survivor because there was little doubt that they would be next.

Later, they pondered how the survivor would justify the deaths of three people. Perhaps their lives weren't in jeopardy. Perhaps they should have stayed to prevent a murder. But at that moment, fleeing seemed the only option, and they increased their speed until exhaustion brought them to a walk.

They moved ahead side by side, catching their breath. They heard faint echoes of the horrific struggle that took place at the rail. The prospect that one of the men would be dead in a matter of moments was terrifying.

Hannah stopped and faced the direction from which they'd come. "Should we go back?"

"And do what?!"

"I don't know! It doesn't feel right just running away like this."

Job hesitated. "How do we know what the struggle is about? Do we know if they're armed? Do we know if one of them is trying to protect us from being hurt or killed? If that's the case, which one is it? What if the struggle is just between the two of them and we're just side players?" he said. "I don't know who taunted us with the checks. There was something about him that I've never seen in anyone before."

"Evil," Hannah said softly. "He is evil."

"Yes, he is evil. But what makes you think the other man is any better? The good guys don't usually hide then pounce on someone at the last minute trying to kill them. We need to find a place to sit tight until nightfall," Job said, then murmured, "If there is such a place. I have no idea where we'll go when it's dark."

"We're miles from anywhere and the nights are cold. There's no food or water."

"Would you rather be cold and hungry or dead?"

Hannah dropped her head. "You're right. We'll keep walking."

Chapter 5

Suddenly, the woods became quiet. The only audible sounds were the birds singing and the crunching of their feet. The absence of noise was infinitely more intimidating than listening to the struggle. The survivor had won. The loser was dead. The two increased their pace.

Moments later, they spotted something looming through the growth. It was large and white. They altered their direction and shortly stood in front of it. The words "Bedford County Maintenance Building" were written above the door.

"Probably locked," Job said.

"Probably, but let's try anyway."

When they couldn't gain access through the door, they walked around the building, looking for an entryway.

Standing in front of the door once again, Hannah turned to Job. "We'll have to break a window. That's the only way to get in here."

They chose a window in the back that appeared to be the easiest to climb through. An unsettling silence surrounded them. How far would the sound of broken glass carry? It was during that period of hesitation that they heard something or someone moving through the brush.

"This way," Job whispered, and they slid away, hiding behind a mound of rocks placed there when the ground was excavated years ago. It was covered with moss and blended in perfectly with its surroundings. They crouched low, not daring to peek through a crevasse in the rocks.

Footsteps walked slowly around the building, then circled the building one more time. They heard the survivor try each window. All was securely locked. Satisfied that the young people he pursued couldn't possibly be inside the building, he moved on. His search grew ever wider till he reached the place where they were hidden. Darkness had become their friend and they were invisible. Eventually, the survivor left.

Even then, Job and Hannah remained where they were. What seemed an eternity later, they heard a car start. Was it the car that brought them from Bedford or the other one? And would it return?

The two young people waited. When they felt safe leaving the security of their hiding place behind the rocks, they waited still longer. It was completely dark when they crept out from behind the rocks.

Job broke the window, slid his hand through the opening, and unlocked it. The window hadn't been opened in years and it took both of them pressing upward till it gave way. Job, being taller, intertwined his fingers and Hannah used them as a step up, then slid over the window sill. Job followed and the window was closed.

Moments ago, darkness had been their friend. Now it was their adversary. Fearful of tripping over an unseen object, they edged along the wall until they came to the front. They positioned themselves on either side of the door, using their hands to search for a light switch. Once the light was on, their level of anxiety doubled. They felt exposed. Even though the maintenance building was some distance from the edge of the cliff where the ruins lay below, they felt vulnerable. Worse yet, they felt utterly alone.

They split up and quickly assessed what resources were available. Hannah came to a door and opened it. Her fingers found a light switch. Quickly surveying the room, she said, "We can hide in here."

Job turned off the main switch and walked toward Hannah, who was backlit against the light behind her. "Good. No windows," he said, then closed the door.

It appeared to be a kitchenette with basic supplies for the workers during the busy season, which would start within the next few weeks. A small refrigerator, microwave, miniature sink, table and four chairs were packed into the space. Everything they needed to survive. But had the water been turned off, and was there even a morsel of food left over from the previous season?

Hannah held her breath as she turned on the tap. Water. They took glasses out of the cabinet and filled them, surprised at their level of thirst.

There were several cans of soup and beef stew, applesauce, and peaches left from the previous season. They collapsed onto chairs and ate their meager dinner. Slowly, their adrenaline returned to normal levels and blessed numbness took its place.

Yet, while Hannah's head bowed over her food, Job observed her. He observed her facial features. Was there any resemblance between them besides their hair which could be manufactured with the aid of a bottle? She seemed tense even though they were safe. She appeared oblivious to her surroundings, then murmured, "I wonder which one was killed?"

What an odd question. "Does it matter?" Job said.

Hannah realized her musings were said aloud. "Oh, no, it doesn't matter." But that faraway look returned to her eyes. Was she worried about herself or who the survivor was?

Chapter 6

Twenty-four hours later, a lawyer called the Bedford Police Department. "This is Jake Prescott from New York," the lawyer said. "I'm Grayson Matthews' attorney. There was an important meeting last night and he missed it. Seems he's gone missing altogether. He flew to Cameron then drove up north to do some fishing of all things. Why he'd want to visit a godforsaken place like that I'll never know. Your town is called—Bedford or something, right?"

Officer Karl Farrell was on duty. He bit back what he would have said off duty. "Yes, our town is called Bedford."

"Right," Jake Prescott said. "I've tried calling Grayson's cell phone but there's been no answer. File a missing person report. Immediately. Can't wait on this."

"Yes, I know he was supposed to be in the area fishing. I can file a missing person report for you."

"Good. This is totally out of character for Grayson and we're concerned. I've chartered a small plane. Should be in, uh, Bedford in a couple of hours. I'll stay at the same hotel as Grayson is—or was, depending on how things are. I'll stop by as soon as I get settled."

"All right, we'll expect you later today, Mr. Prescott," Karl said. He leaned back in his chair. Bedford County didn't get many celebrity-level people making their way through the area. The few that visited left the same way they arrived—alive.

As promised, Jake Prescott walked briskly through the door later that day, every inch the lawyer accustomed to being given every courtesy. He wore his New York attire meant to impress: three-piece business suit, white shirt with gold cufflinks, and a subtle kerchief in his breast pocket. "Just checking in," he said dismissively. He straightened his tie and sniffed in disdain as his eyes swept the small area surrounding Officer Karl Farrell's desk.

Karl Farrell had seen human behavior at its best, worst, and everything in between. He'd dealt with the likes of the Jake Prescotts of this world. "Filed the missing person report after you called. We'll keep in touch with you."

"I'm sure you will, Officer Farrell," Mr. Prescott said, glancing at the name on the desk. "I've checked in at that hotel. They can't tell me a single thing about Grayson. Any place serve good coffee in this town?" he said as if he were asking the impossible.

Karl nodded through the window. "Teddy's Café across the street."

Jake Prescott arched a doubtful eyebrow as he followed the officer's gaze. "I'll give it a try," he sighed, then took out a business card, laid it carelessly on the desk, and exited the door sixty seconds after he arrived.

He crossed the street, shoved his way past a regular customer and waited to be seated.

Teddy witnessed the scene and decided not to make an issue of it. The man was new in the area. Just passing through no doubt. "Table for one or are you expecting someone?" he said to the man's chin.

"I'm alone," Jake Prescott replied, looking over Teddy's head.

"Any seating preference?"

"Table by the window is fine." After he was seated, he refused the menu with a sweep of his hand. "Coffee. Black."

Teddy left the table and deliberately sat his regular customer waiting at the door, then took her order before brewing one cup of coffee. "Here you are," he said pleasantly through gritted teeth.

"Right. Don't go far. If it's good, I'll order another cup."

"It's my café so everything is good. And I'm never far away," Teddy said.

Jake Prescott stared out the window as he sipped his coffee, hiding the smile that was sure to crease his lips if he wasn't careful. He had made the desired impression. Now he needed to maintain it.

Chapter 7

It had been a somewhat tedious afternoon for Cynthia Treadwell. She'd been shopping downtown Bedford, searching for just the right gift for her third son, Bobby. He lived out west. If she didn't mail it today, the gift would arrive after his birthday, and that simply would not do. Having found what she was looking for, she stopped at the post office and stood in an unbearably long line while people shifted their weight from one foot to the other.

An eternity later, she slid behind the wheel of her rather ancient car and headed for home, where she'd treat herself to a nice, hot cup of tea and a slice of chocolate cake before driving to the ruins east of town for an early evening photoshoot. That vision evaporated when she realized she'd used the last drop of milk for her morning tea. No use whining about it. She'd make a quick detour, buy the milk, and be on her way.

She turned left at the next intersection and pulled into the last parking space at Crandall's Corner Market. Walking through the door, she witnessed a scene identical to the post office.

Mr. Crandall was positively run off his feet and appeared oddly distracted. His assistant, Robbie, was nowhere in sight. After gathering her bottle of milk, Miss Treadwell once again stood in line. While Mr. Crandall rang up each customer's purchase, a middle-aged, well-dressed woman leaned into the counter, wanting to know where the liquid peppermint was. Having a bit of trouble with the mice getting into her house. She'd moved in across the street recently and heard it was just the thing to discourage them.

"I'll show her," Miss Treadwell said. Mr. Crandall nodded his thanks. The woman trailed along after her down aisle three.

"Oh, yes, thank you so much," the woman said. She had a pleasant face. Brown hair sprinkled with gray. Almost as tall as Miss Treadwell and just as slender. She wore black slacks, a white shirt, and a red jacket. People of her caliber rarely settled in Bedford.

As Miss Treadwell resumed her place in line, she wondered where the woman had come from and did she plan to settle here.

Once again, the woman stood before her asking where she might find another item which required yet another trip down a different aisle. She had positively no objections, but where on earth was Robbie? This was his job.

The line grew ever shorter until Miss Treadwell stood at the counter. She placed her single bottle of milk on the counter and reached for her billfold. "You're busy this afternoon, Mr. Crandall," she said, subtly referring to his absent assistant.

Mr. Crandall shook his head as he rang up the sale. "No idea where Robbie is. He's never been late before, let alone not shown up at all.

Hasn't been to work for two days now. I called Helen this morning. That's his landlady. Just lives down the street," he said, then stood with her change in his hand as he stared vacantly out the window. "Helen said she hasn't seen him. No idea where he is."

"Two days? And no idea where he is? That is odd. Did his landlady mention whether he's disappeared before?"

"Helen said he's never done this before. He's a thoughtful kid." Mr. Crandall's face was a study in worry rather than irritation. "What if he's hurt and needs help?" he murmured to himself, forgetting he had a customer in front of him waiting for her change.

Miss Treadwell forgot about her tea and cake and joined Mr. Crandall inside his circle of worry. "Should you call the police?"

Mr. Crandall turned at the sound of her voice. "I've been thinking about that all day. I don't want to get Robbie in trouble in case he's out having a good time. No doubt he'll show up tomorrow," he said doubtfully. He handed her the change, but his mind was in a fluid state of indecision. "I know Jody down at the police station. Stops in here a good bit. Maybe I'll give her a ring sometime today."

"Yes, Jody is very nice. She's a steady customer?"

"Yep, faithful customer. Lives a couple of blocks away. Just down the street from Robbie."

"I see," Miss Treadwell said. "Consider calling Jody. They have resources to find people."

She unlocked the car door and slid behind the wheel. After starting the car, she saw someone leave the corner store. It was the woman she'd helped a few moments ago. That was odd. The woman only had two items. Where was she during her conversation with Mr. Crandall?

She watched the woman cross the street and walk into one of the rowhouses. Interesting.

Miss Treadwell drove home all thoughts of tea and cake forgotten as she continued to worry about the young man who had "never been late before, let alone not shown up."

Arriving home, she walked into a room then forgot why she was there. Normally an organized, efficient woman, she had a rather stern conversation with herself, then changed clothes, gathered her camera, phone, and purse, and drove to the ruins east of town. But by then, it was growing dark.

She'd never been to the ruins and glanced at the directions her neighbor, Myrtle Martin, had given her. Turn right onto Cliff Road. The ruins are on the left just before the lane leading up to the cliff.

Parking her car in the east lot, she made her way through the tall, damp grass toward the ruins. There were three old buildings left to decay and despair within twenty minutes of her house in Bedford. Why had she never visited this charming place before?

She loved the morning light, but decided the magic hour, that wonderful hour before sunset, might be perfect for taking shots of these sad relics of a long-forgotten past. Having gotten such a late start, she regretted there were only a few minutes left till sunset.

The camera strap rested comfortably on her shoulder as she reached the first of three buildings. She studied it, searching for the perfect angle. As her eyes drifted from one spot to the next, she considered what to prepare for dinner the following evening when two of her boys arrived at six.

Kneeling and sitting on the ground was a rather dirty job, which is why she dressed in an ancient pair of slacks and shoes. She knelt on one knee to capture a shot of the last moments of light reflecting in the broken glass of two windows. It was then her peripheral vision sensed motion about two hundred feet behind the buildings and she turned her head.

He moved rapidly through the darkened shadows. That's how she knew someone was walking along the path below a wall that rose sharply behind the ruins. Had he remained stationary, he would have blended in with the surroundings. It was an unsettling feeling thinking she was safely alone only to see someone. Had he seen her? She thought not—hoped not.

Suddenly, Miss Treadwell felt vulnerable. There was a certain charm in being alone with the mystique of the ruins as darkness settled around her that would be lost had she brought someone with her. Yet that mystique quickly evolved to concern, even worry. She was alone in a deserted place with someone making his way along a path she hadn't noticed upon her arrival.

He disappeared behind a line of scraggly shrubs. In the growing darkness, it was difficult to tell where the shrubs ended. She waited, hoping to hear the sound of a car starting. Perhaps, like her, he was here to take in the mesmerizing effect of the ruins. If only she could convince herself of that. It was the rapidity and purpose with which he moved that brought doubt to her mind.

Chapter 8

Miss Treadwell waited for someone to appear, perhaps shouting a greeting so as not to alarm her. But the man had vanished. Should she leave? Squaring her shoulders, she halfheartedly decided she hadn't come all this way to be intimidated by a man walking in the shadows.

Having decided to remain a few more minutes, she moved on to the second building one hundred feet from where she stood. Even though it was growing a bit dark, a silhouette can make for an interesting photo. She made her way through the tall grass then stopped short. Someone was already there. Was it the same man she saw walking along the pathway? How could he have arrived there so quickly? He was seated on the third of six steps leading up to the front door.

The man's elbows rested on his knees and his face was buried in his hands. Was he merely tired or resting? Again Miss Treadwell's instinct was to return to her car and leave immediately. But an overwhelming curiosity kept her in place. She studied the young man, for even in the dim light she could see he was young. He appeared to be in deep contemplation, or was it anguish? Somehow his overall affect lent itself to worry rather than fatigue. Or was she reading too much into it?

He lifted his head and looked straight ahead as if gazing intently at something. Miss Treadwell followed his gaze, but as darkness progressively enveloped them, he didn't appear to be looking at anything in particular. Meditating? Soul searching, perhaps?

She wanted very badly to capture this man's mood. What would she title it? The Man at the Ruins? It would become part of her private collection. With very little light remaining, his expression would be somewhat vague. It was his body language that spoke so loudly of what she hoped to capture.

She dropped to one knee and partially rotated her lens to bring him closer into view. Although his features were somewhat blurred, he appeared to be in a somber, pondering frame of mind which would add enormous visual interest. Was she being intrusive? He couldn't object if he never found out. In any case, the photos would be for her viewing alone. One could justify nearly everything if couched in the right terms.

What was left of the light was behind him, so all that would be visible was his outline. An outline of a man sitting on cracked steps at the sight of a ruin. Perfect. He'd never know and couldn't possibly object. She took two shots as he changed his position, then opened her display panel. Yes, very nicely silhouetted.

She rose to her feet, lifted the camera to her eye and rotated the lens to the maximum degree it was capable, drawing the man's profile closer. She pressed halfway down on the shutter button, which brought the subject into partial focus. As she pressed down on the shutter button, the man turned his head, looking directly into the camera just as she completed the shot. The look on his face was difficult to interpret. Was it anger, fear, or perhaps relief, even hope? Now, why had she added relief and hope to the equation? Whatever his emotions, she became acutely aware that she was the cause of them. She was also acutely aware that he was rising from his seat and quickly descending the steps.

There was something about the desperate hurriedness with which he moved toward her that Miss Treadwell found frightening. At seventy, she was still slender, agile, and spry. And it was time to use those gifts to leave immediately. Pivoting quickly, she made for her car in record time. Behind, she heard his voice calling to her, but in her rush to escape, she didn't internalize his words. Sliding behind the wheel, she started the old car, and pulled away.

This feeling of relief was an odd one. She couldn't quite put her finger on it. He was just a man who had taken a walk and chose to sit on the steps of a ruined building. But there was something about his reaction when he saw her. Most people would either speak to her, turn their head, or get up and walk away. He appeared almost desperate. But why? Good heavens! How could one feel desperately worried about a senior citizen innocently taking photos just after sunset?

Miss Treadwell was a somewhat cautious driver, "somewhat" in that it very much depended on the circumstances. Evidently this circumstance called for significant pressure on the gas pedal. She glanced every few seconds in her rear-view mirror as she raced along Cliff Road.

In less than a moment, she saw headlights behind her in the distance. Well, after all, this was a public highway. Anyone with a driver's license was free to travel on it. Somehow, she found this less than comforting, perhaps because she also knew this road was rarely used by anyone but those wishing to see the ruins. In fact, if her memory served her well, she'd heard that the road came to a dead end three hundred feet beyond the place where she'd parked.

Was it her imagination or was the car gaining on her? Really! Had she succumbed to that crippling emotion so many of her older friends had contracted? Fear of everything. Yet her eyes had not betrayed her as they flicked back and forth from the windshield to the rear-view mirror. He was there and still closing in on her.

Unconsciously, her mind shifted to survival mode. A turn appeared just ahead. Miss Treadwell pressed on the brakes just enough to negotiate the turn but squealing tires and sliding halfway through it was the price she paid. Within half a mile, another turn presented itself.

A house was just ahead. There were no lights shining through the windows. Were they not at home or hadn't they turned them on yet? Survival mode meant taking risks. She pulled into the driveway and didn't stop until she reached a shed beyond the house. Turning off her lights and shutting off the ignition, she waited a moment while she considered her next move.

She grabbed her phone, bolted from the car, and hid behind the shed. With trembling fingers, she punched in the first three numbers of Ralph's phone. Her head dropped. He was having dinner with Sam that night. She could call her other son. It was still the rush hour at Teddy's Café, which was across the street from the police station where Ralph worked. It wasn't as though she had an accident or was in imminent danger. After all, people head in the same direction all the time. No, she'd see this through alone somehow.

Hope faded as a vehicle slowly turned onto the same road. Was that the car following her? She couldn't be sure because the headlights in her rear-view mirror denied her the opportunity to identify it.

The car appeared to be driverless. She realized either the windows were darkened or the moonless night prevented her from seeing the interior of the vehicle. All she saw was something small, black, and square moving slowly down the road. No expert on cars, that was the best she could come up with. In any event, it was well past sunset by now, so her car would appear to be a dark object in the driveway. Hopefully he'd think it belonged to the owner of the house.

The vehicle slowed down as it neared the driveway where she stood. The house was dark. She looked over her shoulder for a possible means of escape, but there was only a vast void with nowhere to hide. Then another thought came to the forefront. Perhaps it was the owner of the house returning. But as the vehicle drove slowly past the driveway, the initial thought gave way to another one. Perhaps the person lived farther down the road.

Patience was a virtue Cynthia Treadwell strove to master. Sadly, she often failed. Today she conquered her impulse to jump in her car and bolt for home. Moments later, she was grateful, because the very same vehicle returned driving just as slowly. Had he returned because he'd seen a car parked in the driveway?

No streetlights, no houselights. She felt the night closing in on her. She felt trapped. How long should she wait to make sure he didn't return? Fifteen minutes. If he didn't return within fifteen minutes, she'd leave.

Yet when the fifteen minutes eventually passed, she wasn't at all sure where she was. She'd executed turns in a state of panic. She'd never been on these back country roads before. Should she turn left or right out of the driveway? If she got lost, these country roads were notorious for dead zones. What if she became completely lost and couldn't call anyone? Chiding herself again for acting every inch the older lady she pretended not to be, she got in her car and backed out onto the road.

As she made her way to the main road, her eyes were fixed on her rear-view mirror as much as the windshield. No headlights trailed behind her.

But what she didn't see was a vehicle enveloped in darkness tailing her from the moment she pulled onto Cliff Road until she turned into a driveway in Bedford.

Chapter 9

Unable to go home just yet, she pulled into the driveway of her next-door neighbor and parked beside the sidewalk.

Myrtle's eyes widened in surprise. "Cynthia, are you all right? You look like something the cat dragged in. Come into the kitchen and I'll brew us a nice hot pot of tea. Just the thing," she said. "You look pale as a ghost. Not that I've ever seen one, mind you. Where have you been?"

"Taking photos, out by the...."

"Well, never mind. You're here now and I'll have you right as rain soon enough."

Myrtle was six inches shorter, thirty pounds heavier, and eight years older than Miss Treadwell. Faithfully attending yoga sessions three times each week had done little to improve her strength or stability. But it gave her an incomparable opportunity to ferret out local information. What Myrtle Martin didn't know about the goings-on in Bedford wasn't worth knowing.

At seventy-eight, she shuffled along in her worn-down slippers a lot slower and with less assuredness, but her mind was as sharp as anyone her age had a right to expect. The pockets in her faded bathrobe had holes in them which she found inconvenient, but we are all inconvenienced by something, she always said. Slipping a comforting arm around her neighbor, she led her into the kitchen, patting her back the entire way. Once there, she bade Cynthia to sit and rest.

Famous for keeping everyone up to date on the latest news, Myrtle put the kettle on the stove to boil while she prattled on about the neighborhood doings. "Had time to read the evening paper, Cynthia? One of those big shots from New York flew into Cameron then came up to Bedford for a bit of fishing or something. Got himself lost. There's a lot of buzz about it. Name's Grayson Matthews or something like that. No photo of him. Don't know how we're supposed to be on the lookout for somebody if they don't put a photo in the newspaper."

Cynthia's mind was still on the man she saw at the ruins and the vehicle that followed her. "Well, no, Myrtle. I wasn't home most of the day."

"Went to my yoga class today," Myrtle said as she poured boiling water into the teapot. "Someone joined our little group a week or so ago."

"How nice," Miss Treadwell murmured vaguely.

"Yes, Helen brought her new neighbor to class. Moved into one of those rowhouses across from Crandall's Corner Market. You know where I mean, Cynthia."

Miss Treadwell looked up. "Mr. Crandall? Oh, yes. I shop there quite often."

"You never know how somebody new is going to work out. But Helen's neighbor seems nice enough. Didn't say much except to ask when class actually started," Myrtle said, then paused. "Well, some days we get to yoga and some days we don't. You know how it is, Cynthia."

"Oh, yes, I definitely know how it is."

Myrtle's brows drew together. "Now, what is her name? Well, I'll find out tomorrow."

"I'm sure she's very nice," Miss Treadwell repeated for lack of anything else to say.

"Now where was I?" Myrtle said. "Oh, yes. That Matthews fellow. Word has it he didn't show up at his hotel for the last couple of nights and everybody's in an absolute uproar about it."

"That is a bit odd. And no one's seen him since then?"

"Not hide nor hair. At least that's what I heard from the girls at yoga."

"Well, we all need our time to get away and not be bothered by anyone."

"Not if you're Grayson Matthews, you don't. The public starts to worry about you."

"Do the authorities think something's happened to him?"

Myrtle picked up the paper and placed it on the table in front of her next-door neighbor. "No idea. You'll probably hear all about it tomorrow night when Ralph and Teddy come to dinner. They're still coming to dinner, aren't they? Ralph's not too busy, is he?"

A tired hand shoved the evening newspaper aside. "Did I mention the boys are coming to dinner?" Miss Treadwell said, knowing full well she hadn't said a word about it.

"Oh, my dear. Common knowledge they come every Wednesday,"

Myrtle said. "I suppose Ralph will be knee-deep in the investigation. Missing person of that caliber. You probably won't see much of him for a while, I suspect."

"What do you know about him?"

"Just what I told you. He's one of those big shots from New York," Myrtle said. "Landed at the airport in Cameron, drove up here to Bedford to do some fishing, then got lost. Don't know what fish he expected to catch in these parts. Now nobody seems to know where he is," Myrtle said. She set the tea tray in the middle of the table, poured tea for both of them, and placed the milk jug beside her neighbor. "Of course, he hasn't been gone that long, but big shots aren't allowed to go missing for very long."

"Maybe he needed a break from the tedium of being a big shot," Miss Treadwell said, in an offhanded manner. "He'll turn up when he's ready."

"Last I heard, nobody knows if he even went fishing." The first hot cup was consumed in silence before Myrtle added, "Strange that an important man like Grayson Matthews would wander off somewhere without telling anyone. Don't you think?"

"If he truly wants to be alone, it's rather difficult to do so if he tells everyone where he is going," Miss Treadwell said. "I suspect he'll turn up when he's good and ready."

"The question isn't so much whether he'll turn up. The question is, will he be found alive or otherwise?"

"Alive or dead?"

"Well, he may have decided to do himself in. You know, end it all. That sort of thing."

48

"I see," Miss Treadwell said, taking another sip. "Unhappy? Perhaps he was unhappy and saw this as his only way out?"

"Don't suicide cases write a letter explaining why they're doing this? Surely he would have left a note."

"Well, I don't think we should convict an innocent man until we know more of the facts."

"Ralph is a police officer. That's something he would say. He looks for ironclad alibis, DNA samples, fingerprints and who knows what else," Myrtle said, sipping her tea while she continued to think. "You're right. Best not make judgments about it till the facts are in. But I'll be shocked if they declare it a case of suicide."

"You're saying it's murder?" Miss Treadwell said. "The poor man has only been missing a short time. Best not jump to staggering conclusions yet."

"You never know about these things, Cynthia. If he's missing because he's been murdered, then there's a murderer running loose somewhere here in Bedford."

Chapter 10

After hearing that pronouncement, Miss Treadwell needed another sustaining cup of tea. "Why on earth do you think a man who's gone fishing because he wants a break from the overwhelming burden of being a big shot would turn up dead?"

"Just a hunch." Myrtle shrugged her shoulders then changed the subject. "Where did you take pictures tonight?"

Miss Treadwell's mind and body were utterly drained of energy. However, she knew if she hesitated with her response, it would be all over town within twenty-four hours that her poor, dear neighbor was finally losing it. "The ruins east of town. Nearly dark when I got there, so the last few shots weren't very good. A bit blurred in fact." She hesitated, then felt the need to unburden her fear and anxiety onto someone's shoulders. Myrtle listened intently as Miss Treadwell relived her experience. As they did an hour ago, her hands began to tremble; not violently, but noticeably when she lifted her teacup to her lips.

The observant type, Myrtle noticed every inflection in her neighbor's voice and the slight tremor in her hands. If a trifle overenthusiastic when it came to minding everyone else's business, she was also compassionate. "I don't scare all that easily and neither do you, Cynthia. But I have to say what you described would have frightened me, too. Don't like people chasing me in the middle of nowhere after dark. Had your phone I suppose."

"Yes, but it was impossible to call anyone while I was careening down the road. And once I stopped at that deserted house, I remembered Ralph was having dinner with Sam, and Teddy would be very busy at his cafe. I decided I could work through it alone. And, as you see, I did."

"Samantha McKean. She's one of the lab technicians at the crime lab, isn't she?"

"Yes, that's where Sam works."

The two women sipped silently, immersed in their own thoughts. Myrtle had already come to a definite conclusion but wasn't at all sure her neighbor was in a receptive frame of mind to hear it. However, nothing ventured.... "You know what they say when you fall off a bicycle or a horse."

The transition from her experience an hour ago and falling off bicycles and horses eluded her. "Remind me."

"Have to get right back on."

"I'm still not following you, Myrtle."

"Very simple, Cynthia. You need to make another trip to the ruins in broad daylight and spend a little time there. Walk around the buildings." When her neighbor's reaction lacked overwhelming enthusiasm, she added, "There's a cliff above the ruins. Ever walked along it?"

Miss Treadwell wasn't partial to heights. "No. Is there something I should know about it?"

"Beautiful views. You can see Muddy Creek and beyond from there. I'm no photographer but I'll wager you'd get some great photos up there."

"I suspect early morning would be best," Miss Treadwell murmured. "How early?"

Miss Treadwell raised an eyebrow. "How early?"

"That's what I said. How early?"

"Well, if I were to take shots overlooking a valley, I'd probably want to be there about seven thirty."

"Hm," Myrtle said.

It had been a tediously long day. She'd been chased by a car and now Myrtle was determined to help her overcome her rather traumatic experience. Her neighbor truly had the best of intentions, but Miss Treadwell had maxed out on the dear soul for one night. It was presently going on nine o'clock, which was very near her bedtime. "Time to get this aching body into a hot tub with something bubbly and smelling of lavender," she said. "Thank you so much for the tea, Myrtle."

"Yes, well, you've had a positively grinding day, Cynthia. A hot bath will do you a world of good."

Miss Treadwell made her way to the car parked at the end of Myrtle's sidewalk. It was a slow, contemplative walk as she thought of the man sitting on the steps at the ruins who appeared distressed. Or was she overreacting to this, just as Myrtle had dramatized the disappearance of the "big shot"? She pondered both issues as she backed out of the driveway.

In less than thirty seconds, she pulled into her garage. Searching through her purse for the keys to the backdoor, she stopped and lifted her head. She'd fished inside her purse as she sat in her car outside Crandall's Corner Market. The woman who needed liquid peppermint walked across the street and into a rowhouse. Could she be the woman who joined Myrtle's yoga class? Probably not. Fatigue overcame curiosity and she let herself into her house, then leaned against the closed door.

Heading down the hallway to place her purse and camera in the closet, she saw the Bedford Evening News lying on the floor. The girl who delivered the newspaper always slid the newspaper through the mail slot where the mail used to be delivered. What had Myrtle said about the article concerning the man's disappearance being in the newspaper? Well, it could wait till the following morning. By then, he may very well have returned from his fishing trip. Myrtle and her friends at the yoga class would suffer disappointment and be forced to find something else to focus on.

After her long, hot, therapeutic bath, Miss Treadwell was certain she'd fall directly to sleep. An hour later, she still tossed and turned. By midnight, she drifted into the kind of restless sleep where dreams take hold.

Unpleasant dreams bedeviled her that night. In her dream, a light shone briefly on her closed lids. She tightened them and turned her head in the opposite direction.

Rolling over in bed, her eyes opened halfway. There was a strip of light shining on the wall. It was coming from her window. Her bedside clock read three o'clock. Curiosity won out. She left the warmth of her bed, slid her feet into slippers, her arms through her bathrobe, and padded over to the window.

A dark shadow of a car was advancing slowly down Myrtle's driveway. But the lights had been turned off. Who in the world would be pulling into Myrtle's driveway at this unseemly hour? Was the light shining in her eyes a dream or had it been that car? If it had been the car, they must have been turned on a moment ago. She stood staring through her bedroom window, expecting the car to back up and leave. But it didn't. It stopped and parked at the end of Myrtle's sidewalk where she'd parked earlier.

Miss Treadwell knew very little about cars. But she understood shapes. The shape of that vehicle was identical to the one that followed her seven hours ago.

Chapter 11

Miss Treadwell grabbed her camera from the hall closet and made her way to the living room window. Rotating the lens, she drew the vehicle closer to her eye but couldn't see anyone inside. The windows were as dark as the vehicle itself. She shot a few photos even though they're always blurred through glass. With the minimal light provided by a sliver of moon, all that appeared on her display panel was a rectangular shadow.

She expected the car to leave, but it remained. Someone slipped out of the passenger side and hurried to the back of the house, while Miss Treadwell took photos in rapid succession. The mystery visitor was a dark running figure until they reached the side of the house. There was enough ambient light from the moon that the outline of a woman was visible against white siding.

The woman returned shortly, but the light from the moon wasn't sufficient, and the drainpipe that extended into the grass went unseen.

She tripped and fell, then rose to a sitting position and reached inside her pocket, withdrew a tissue, and closed her fingers around it. Slowly, she rose and made her way to the car.

There were two people in that car. Possibly more. One of them was injured, if only slightly.

Within seconds, the car backed out onto the road. Instead of leaving, it pulled over to the side and appeared to wait. But why? Wait for what?

The car could pull away at any time. Why hadn't Miss Treadwell rushed outside immediately? The fact that she'd been asleep and her thinking was a bit muddled was positively no excuse.

Pressing soundlessly through the backdoor, she stopped at the edge of the garage, leveled her camera, and snapped four shots. On the other side of the garage, she took four more photos. Opening her display panel, she knew this was useless. Parked between streetlights, the car was shrouded in darkness. Or was it the vehicle itself that was dark and therefore difficult to photograph? The images could be edited, but she wasn't sure the editing process would lighten them enough because the vehicle absolutely blended into the night.

A moment later, the driver pulled soundlessly away.

Miss Treadwell leaned against the garage. Was she overreacting? Was she still under the fearful spell created by the man at the ruins? When he realized she was looking at him, was his reaction completely outside the realm of normalcy? Any illusions she'd had that he was merely driving in the same direction had disappeared. He was most assuredly following her.

There was something working its way to the forefront of her mind. Ralph had talked about it after dinner two weeks ago. Blood. There was something about blood samples that he mentioned that night. DNA. It involved collecting a sample and sending it off to some lab in Cameron just south of Bedford.

She reviewed that fifteen-second frame. The woman fell, reached inside a pocket, and pulled out a tissue or handkerchief because she was bleeding. Was it possible she bled on something that could be collected as a sample?

With only three hours' sleep under her belt, Miss Treadwell dashed into the house, collected a pair of Ralph's evidence gloves, a baggy, and a flashlight. Scissors? Better to take too much than too little.

Armed with evidence-gathering equipment and her camera slung over her shoulder, she ventured through the row of peonies that peeked through the ground and divided the two properties. When she reached the spot she thought the woman fell, she shone the flashlight directly in front of her feet to avoid destroying the evidence she hoped to gather.

Perhaps she needed to find the drainpipe that extended through the grass first. Stepping back, she tracked the light across the grass until she found the drainpipe. Slowly, she crept forward, careful to maintain a safe distance. And there it was. How could she have forgotten? Myrtle had planted a perennial bed along the side of the house. In order to define it, she'd also placed bricks along its edge. Striving to be unique, she didn't press the bricks parallel to the ground. They were positioned in a line that zigzagged. The edges weren't necessarily sharp unless something fell on them.

Everything presented itself as mostly black and white. She'd have to look at each individual brick closely for a color that varied slightly. When she came upon it, she leaned in closer. Yes, she could see a slight variation in color. She could also see that this particular brick was out of alignment with its neighbors.

Now, the question was, did she dare chip off a corner of Myrle's brick? She sat back on her heels for a moment, debating the issue. Ultimately, she decided on the greater good. Donning the evidence gloves, she took the scissors out of her bathrobe pocket and hacked away at the darkened area until the corner came away, hoping the entire time that Myrtle was a sound sleeper. She dropped the sliver of brick inside the baggie and sealed it. The chipped area was obvious. The only solution was to turn the brick one hundred eighty degrees so the damaged section was buried in the dirt.

Suddenly, she felt chilled to the bone, whether because of the cool night air or the cumulative effect of the day's events. Rising to her feet, she stumbled back to the kitchen where the bright light would determine whether the brick was tainted with blood or something else. Undoubtedly it was just dirt.

Inside the kitchen, the tiniest of smiles creased her lips. Yes, it was blood. The brick was beige, so it allowed for contrast with the redness of the blood. It must have been quite a severe cut for the blood flowed freely enough to create a fairly large, stained area.

Now, what should she do with this for the present? Did it need refrigeration? "Better safe than sorry" had been her lifelong motto. In the heat of the moment, that motto was nearly always cast aside. She wrote the date, time, and location on the baggie, popped it into the refrigerator then put the kettle on to boil. Hot tea would warm her chilled, aching bones.

Sitting at the table moments later, she pondered the events beginning shortly after seven o'clock the previous evening. She arrived at the ruins and began shooting pictures. By seven thirty, she'd worked her way around the first building and part of the second building. When she rounded a corner, a man was sitting on the steps leading up to the front door. He looked despondent. Was that the correct word? Worried, apprehensive, depressed? Difficult to say, but his posture spoke of a man in deep distress. Within a minute of starting her photoshoot, he turned to look at her. He called out, but what he said completely escaped her.

Why was her strongest emotion fear rather than guilt? Why had she fled the area? She knew why: self-preservation. Was the car that followed her the same car she'd just photographed?

Her eyes drifted to the refrigerator where she'd placed the sample. Did the car pulling into Myrtle's driveway and the woman venturing into the backyard have anything to do with what happened at the ruins?

What were they doing next door and what was their intent? Should she call the police? And just what would she say? Someone pulled into my neighbor's driveway, realized they'd made a mistake and left? But just before they left, someone fell, cut her hand and I've now completely contaminated the area by collecting my version of samples.

Was there a sensible explanation for all of this? Had she converted a silly molehill into what appeared to be a mountain? Because that may be exactly what happened. What Miss Treadwell couldn't rationalize was this: if it was a mistake, why had the woman gotten out of the car and run to the back of the house? Miss Treadwell would talk to Ralph and Teddy about it. Sighing, she wasn't at all sure that was a good idea. They'd be worried about her and perhaps a tiny bit disgusted that she'd done something rather foolish on her own—again.

Chapter 12

Leto pulled away from the curb, then said, "We need that camera. Is there an easy way to get into the house?"

"Not easy. But it's possible. She may not realize the significance of the photos she took. If she creates too many waves, we'll decide then," Hannah said. "You're sure you got the right house last night?"

"I'm sure. I followed her from the ruins," he said, then hesitated before revealing his error of judgment. "Look, I panicked and got too close to her."

"What do you mean you 'got too close to her'?"

"She was driving fast. I decided to press harder so I didn't lose her. I needed to know who she was and where she was going. When she turned onto that back road, I let up a little."

Hannah sighed. "Go on."

"There's a sign indicating there's no exit, but she must have missed it. Either that or she lived back there and was headed home."

"Did she see you follow her around the turn?"

"I don't know. I couldn't find her. I knew if she didn't live back there, she'd have to return to Cliff Road at some point. I drove back, turned in the direction of the ruins, and waited for her."

"With your lights off."

"Right," he said. "With my lights off. By the time she came out, I'd nearly given up. I tailed her at a distance and kept my lights off. It took nearly half an hour, but eventually I followed her to her house. She pulled into that driveway. I waited until I was sure she was in the house then pulled forward. Her car was right beside the sidewalk."

"You're sure she didn't see you?"

"I told you, I followed at a distance with my lights off," Leto said in a strained voice. "I'm positive she didn't know she was being followed."

"And you're sure she didn't walk along the path below the cliff and find anything, right?"

Leto's jaw was set. He didn't like being questioned. "I don't know if she walked along the path under the cliff! I'd only moved him fifteen minutes before that. The path is in the back of the ruins. The first time I saw her was when she came around the corner of one of the buildings."

"Couldn't you have waited to move him after you found all the pieces? Do you know how many are left?"

"I've pasted together all the pieces of the checks I've found. There can't be more than half a dozen left. If I can't find them, I doubt if anyone else will either."

"Are you willing to stake your life on it?"

"Okay, okay! I'll go back early tomorrow morning and look again."

"Good. We don't want someone else to find them. They probably won't know their significance. Once the police are involved, they'll comb that area and find what you didn't."

"Do you think I don't know that?" he snapped.

"Okay, don't get upset. I hope you find them, because sometime soon, the police will be swarming all over the place and we won't have a chance to go back. Why didn't you wait until you'd found all the pieces?"

"Look," Leto began. "Earlier in the day I was up there searching and someone was walking her dog. The dog was off leash and stopped to nose around the underbrush where I'd hidden him. I was terrified the woman would be curious enough to see what her dog was doing. But all she did was call him and keep going. I figured the next time something like that happened, we might not be so lucky. I know we needed more time. But the risk was too great. I waited till there was enough daylight that I could still see but darkness wasn't far away either. Okay?"

"Okay, okay. Just asking," Hannah said. "Do you know who the woman you followed back from the ruins is?"

"Myrtle Martin," he said. "I checked her mailbox after she was in the house. She'd put a letter in there addressed to someone. It had a preprinted sticker for the return address, so her name was clear."

She stared out the side window while he cooled off. "What about the house you rented? Have you checked on it? Did the real estate agent make all the modifications you asked for?"

"Yes, I've checked the house I rented and all the modifications have been made," Leto said. "The rental agent wasn't willing to do that until I doubled the commission he normally receives."

There were two other critical issues that plagued Hannah's mind.

"You said this Myrtle Martin was taking photos when you were at the ruins. Do you think she took a photo of you, and would she recognize you if she did?"

"I don't know. Don't see how," Leto said. "It was almost dark when I saw her walking around snapping photos. All I saw was a dark outline of a woman. I figure if it was too dark for me to recognize her, it was too dark for her to recognize me, too. Any photo she took of me would be just another dark outline."

"I hope you're right, otherwise all this was for nothing," Hannah said.

"We still have no idea where those two kids are. They can't have just disappeared. For all we know, they may have walked back to town and are spilling everything to the police right now."

"Let's hope they're holed up somewhere."

As the car drew near their next target, Leto glanced at the young woman sitting beside him. "Are you sure you have the key to get into the house?"

"Got the key in my hand. Shouldn't be too difficult to get inside. The landlady is old and lives alone. I'll slip inside, find what I want, and get out," Hannah said. "I won't have any trouble if it's the key to the house."

"The key was in the kid's pocket along with the phone. He didn't have anything else in either pocket except those two things," he said. "Want me to go with you?"

"No; might make too much noise. It's better if I go alone," Hannah said.

"You said it's only a couple of blocks from Crandall's Corner Market, right?"

"Right," Hannah said. "I'll tell you where to turn."

"We can't afford any blood stains while you're there. Is your cut still bleeding?"

Hannah released the pressure which had stopped the initial bleeding and lifted it as they drove past a streetlight. "It's stopped. I'll wrap my hand before I go into the house just to be on the safe side."

"What if you don't find it? Maybe I should go with you."

"No! You'll be in the way. I know where to look. Just sit tight and wait for me."

"What if she wakes up while you're there?"

Hannah stared out the window again while she debated. "Let's just hope she doesn't."

Helen sat by the window for three hours, waiting for Robbie to come home. He didn't owe her an explanation. He rented her upstairs apartment. But she'd come to love this young tenant like a son. So she sat gazing up the street, knowing something had happened, but had no idea what to do about it.

By ten o'clock, she made her way down the hallway to her first-floor bedroom and readied herself for bed. Even in her restless sleep she waited for that turn of the key in the lock and his well-known footsteps climbing the backstairs. Then it came. The sound of the key turning in the lock and footsteps on the backstairs. But they weren't Robbie's footsteps.

The next morning she lay in bed thinking of the dream she'd had the night before. But was it a dream?

Chapter 13

Very early the following morning Miss Treadwell sat at the kitchen table sipping tea and eating her customary two pieces of toast. Normally she slept till eight thirty, but with all that had happened, she found it impossible to linger in bed.

She gazed at the flowered tea cozy that kept the tea inside her teapot wonderfully hot while she considered how to best deal with the events of the previous night. She most certainly needed to explain everything to her neighbor. She wiped her hands on a napkin, then opened the display panel of her camera again. How could anyone make sense out of dark outlines against an even darker background? The shots taken while the woman passed the white siding were good, but only relative to the others, which were nearly indecipherable at three o'clock in the morning.

Putting her camera aside, she poured another cup of tea and reached for last night's newspaper. The headline on the front page didn't say much.

WHEREABOUTS OF GRAYSON MATTHEWS REMAIN UNKNOWN

She'd just done the washing up when the phone rang. "Cynthia?"

"You're up early, Myrtle."

"How would you like to go for a drive?"

"A drive?"

"Yes, today."

Miss Treadwell's heart sank a bit. She was in a reflective mood and wanted to sit and contemplate. Beyond that, she needed to make a phone call and hopefully make a luncheon date with the only person who could help her. But she rallied and said, "Where did you have in mind?"

"Well, I was thinking perhaps the ruins and the surrounding area. You know. What we talked about last night. Getting back on the bicycle or horse. Do you a world of good to get out and see that area in broad daylight. You can put to rest those dreadful images of last night. What do you think?"

"When did you have in mind?" she said, hoping she could talk her into later in the day.

"Nothing like the present."

Miss Treadwell was tired. Tired physically and emotionally. But, after all, her dear neighbor had given her two sustaining cups of tea when she desperately needed them and sympathetically listened to her pour out her worries. "That's very kind of you, Myrtle. It will be nice to get away and not dwell on last night."

"Wonderful!" Myrtle said. "I'll pick you up in ten minutes."

Miss Treadwell had been an unwitting passenger in her car before. "Never mind, I'll drive. Better take a jacket. It's chilly this early in the morning."

She dressed quickly into an old pair of slacks, polo shirt, and walking shoes. After running a comb through her hair, she collected a jacket, camera, phone, and purse, then headed out the backdoor.

Myrtle stood at the end of her sidewalk wearing clothes she'd picked up at a rummage sale ten years ago. She walked around the back of the car, stopped for a moment, then lowered herself onto the passenger seat, clucking her tongue in disapproval. "Cynthia, you really must get that dent in your back fender repaired. Consider the issues. Your car is monstrously old. You're going to have an awful time finding a garage who can match that shade of dark blue."

"I'm sure they'll manage."

"Really, it won't do," Myrtle rattled on. "I suspect every time you look at that dent you remember the day you were hit from behind and run cruelly off the road into a tree. The concussion you suffered was something dreadful. Nobody believed a word you said for a week."

"Yes, well, I survived," Miss Treadwell said, then added quickly, "I have every intention of getting the dent in my back fender repaired. I'm calling the garage this week."

Myrtle nodded her approval. "I hope you brought your camera, Cynthia. We'll have to turn back if you didn't."

"I brought my camera," she said, then moistened her lips. "Myrtle, did you hear a car or see anyone in your backyard last night?"

Myrle turned in her seat. "No. I sleep like the proverbial log. You wouldn't ask me something like that unless there was someone in my backyard last night."

Knowing Myrtle, she should have memorized a script. Except there really wasn't an easy way to tell someone prowlers had invaded her property in the middle of the night.

"A light shone in my face at three o'clock. I really wasn't sleeping well anyway, so it woke me. When I went to the window I saw a car parked beside your sidewalk. A woman jumped out, ran around to the back of your house, then returned to the car. The driver backed out but didn't leave."

"Didn't leave? Just sat there? That's odd."

"I thought so, too. You'd think they'd be in a roaring hurry to get away," Miss Treadwell said. "But it remained for a short time, parked between the street lights. I know virtually nothing about cars, so I really couldn't identify what type it was. Too dark anyway."

When Myrtle didn't respond, Miss Treadwell glanced at her neighbor. She had paled somewhat. It would be especially worrying when one is elderly and alone. "I'm sure it's nothing."

"Oh, I wouldn't be too sure about that. If the woman hadn't gotten out of the car, I might be persuaded they pulled into the wrong house, although that theory is a hard sell at three o'clock in the morning. It has to be more than that," Myrtle said. "Do you see what I mean?"

"I do see what you mean. Perhaps I should have called the police."

"By the time they got to my house, the car would have left," Myrtle replied. "I was in my backyard first thing this morning, checking my daffodils. There wasn't any damage to my property that I could see. So what could they do about it? It was dark, you can't identify them or their car, so it comes to a dead end."

"I suppose you're right." Miss Treadwell withheld the fact that she'd taken photos which she hoped would prove useful if the person she wanted to meet for lunch was available. There wasn't anywhere else to take it so the subject was dropped. Yet it settled in the forefront of their minds, both wondering if this had been an exploratory venture the previous night. And would they be back?

Miss Treadwell retraced the route she'd taken the night before. Her anxiety rose as she turned onto Cliff Road, then rose higher still as she drew closer to the place she'd seen the man sitting on the steps. In the cool light of day, with her neighbor seated beside her, it seemed a bit silly to worry about a car presumably following her which, no doubt, was merely headed in the same direction and most likely got lost. And so what if a man stood up when he saw her? He appeared to be in a rush. Perhaps he was late for an appointment. One can justify nearly everything in life.

She pulled into the same parking space, turned off the ignition, and sat with her hands still gripping the steering wheel as she stared blankly through the windshield.

Myrtle studied her neighbor for a moment. Her demeanor hadn't changed. It was nearly always the same. But there was that underlying tension evidenced by the white knuckles. "Show me the place where the man sat," she said softly. "Let's chase that demon right out of your head."

Miss Treadwell blinked, took her hands off the steering wheel, and got out of the car. Silently, she led the way across the spacious if unkempt lawn until they stood in the spot where she'd taken the three photos. "It was on those steps. I was standing right about here when I saw him." They stood for a moment while the dark memory that held her captive through the night loosened. "Yes, I do feel better. Not completely, but better."

Myrtle patted her neighbor's arm encouragingly. "Let's drive up to the cliff. You can look around and see what photos you want to take."

The women retraced their steps and settled back into the car.

Miss Treadwell turned the car around and said, "Which way to the top of the cliff?"

"Turn left and drive past the ruins. You'll see a narrow lane to the left."

Chapter 14

As he neared the ruins, Leto saw a car up ahead ready to pull out onto the road. He recognized Myrtle Martin's car because his headlights had shone on the back of it as he followed her the previous evening. What were the chances she'd return to the ruins on this particular morning? What possible motive drew her here? And what were the odds that she'd recognize his car? Slim, he hoped. His car had been cloaked in darkness last night.

He sat in a quandary of indecision. He desperately needed to find the remaining pieces of the checks that had been tauntingly tossed in the air the afternoon of the—accident. It was so much easier to rationalize away an accident rather than call it by its legal name.

If Myrtle Martin turned right, she'd reach his car within seconds. There was that off chance she'd recognize his car, but there was no-where to turn around on this narrow road. The fact that he sat in his car two hundred feet from the entrance to the ruins would be completely out of the ordinary. People were naturally curious about things that were out of the ordinary. He felt a sudden dampness on his hands and wiped them on his shirt. But his anxiety quickly turned to surprise because she didn't turn right. She turned left. He closed his eyes momentarily. They'll see the car parked at the top of the ruins. Sighing, he opened his eyes. Someone had to find it sometime. In any case, he doubted she'd question why it was there.

The road came to a dead end a short distance beyond the ruins. The only reason to turn left was if she intended to pull into the lane leading up to the top of the cliff. Did he dare draw closer? Perhaps not. He'd follow from a distance and use the service entrance and park behind the maintenance building which was a distance from the hiking area. What he needed was a permanent solution to an ongoing problem.

Miss Treadwell pulled into a small parking lot. Another car was parked there, but the driver must have gone hiking for there was no one in sight. She'd never been at the top of the cliff, so she allowed Myrtle to lead the way to the cliff's edge in her slow but steady fashion.

Myrtle walked straight to the edge and placed her hands on the rail that kept viewers from accidentally falling over. She seemed transported by the view and Miss Treadwell wasn't inclined to get that close to the drop-off. "I'll just take a walk to see what I can find, Myrtle." Her neighbor didn't reply, so she wandered along the pathway that ran parallel to the drop-off careful to maintain a safe distance from the edge of the cliff.

Early morning and the magic hour before sunset were the best times to take photos. She took off the protective cap that covered the camera's lens, taking several mediocre shots while she inhaled the newness of the day and exhaled the darkness of the previous night.

The views from the top of the cliff were glorious. An entire new area for shooting photos suddenly opened up to her and she found herself unconsciously walking farther from Myrtle and drawing ever closer to the edge to explore the limitless possibilities it offered. In the distance, Muddy Creek meandered through the woods. Just enough time had passed that the trauma of what occurred at Muddy Creek had lessened and she thought of her young friend, Mike. She'd visit him at the hospital later in the week.

As she studied the shots of Muddy Creek on the display panel at the back of her camera, her eyes drifted to the ground in front of her. The grass was uprooted in places and pressed down in others as if there'd been a violent struggle. Her eyes tracked the struggle as it continued to the very edge of the drop-off. Her mind couldn't process what was abundantly clear.

Inching forward till she reached the edge, she grabbed hold of the rail, and forced her eyes to look down. And there it was. The first ten feet formed a steep downward descent. After that, it was a vertical drop to the pathway below. There were broken twigs and branches throughout that first ten feet. Beyond that, there was nothing to grab onto.

Her knuckles grew white as they grasped the rail. She peeled her fingers off the rail and stepped back, casting a glance in the direction from which she'd come. Myrtle was but a dot in the distance.

She refocused her eyes on the ground. The change in the grass was subtle. Patches of the grass had righted themselves for the most part, but the uprooted grass was still visible. And there was quite a lot of it. The broken twigs and slender branches on the ten-foot vertical descent couldn't be spotted unless one was standing right at the edge of the cliff, looking down. But this wasn't obvious to anyone passing by. Something had occurred in this spot fairly recently. Impossible to determine how recent, but grass didn't uproot itself independently. Nor did it uproot itself without a struggle to remain in the ground. Something or someone had disturbed it.

Should she call the police? Was uprooted grass significant enough to call Ralph? Or was she creating another mountain out of a molehill? After all, there may be a very reasonable explanation for this. Somehow, she doubted it.

Lifting her camera, she began to take shots. She took close-ups, stepped back, and took shots using a wide-angle lens. Now the most difficult part. It was necessary to lean against the rail to take photos of the path something took when it fell over the rail to the ground below. If not something then someone. For it was impossible to think otherwise. Needs must. And this was a definite need. She stepped forward, forced her eyes to focus on the vertical drop-off, and took several shots.

Stepping back, she viewed the photos on her display panel. When she reached the shots she'd taken of the ten-foot descent, she focused on one particular item. It looked like the corner of a piece of paper. Yet it wasn't actually paper.

Miss Treadwell returned to the rail again, leaned over, and rotated her lens to the maximum degree it would allow. As she viewed the shot at the maximum setting, she'd been correct. It wasn't merely paper. It looked like the corner of a check. The bottom right-hand corner to be exact. And there were the last two letters of someone's name. The letters were written hurriedly. Scribbled almost, impossible to decipher. What an odd thing to find. Why would someone tear up a check and cast it to the whim of the wind? Seemed rather silly at the time, but she snapped two images of that torn piece of the check.

She checked her watch. It was time to leave, because there was someone she wanted to call, and she wanted to make the call from home. She retraced her steps, pondering what she'd just seen.

Miss Treadwell walked back along the pathway with her head lowered and her camera strap draped over her shoulder. She was deep in thought as she processed what she'd seen and photographed. Were the photos she took evidence that two people struggled, ultimately leading to one of them being forced over the rail? Or perhaps fell over by sheer accident? But that idea was ludicrous.

Through the depths of her thoughts, she heard a sharp cry. Miss Treadwell's head rose. Was it the cry of an animal or human? She waited, but all was quiet. The cry was unsettling and she doubled her pace, reaching the area she'd last seen her neighbor. But where was she?

Chapter 15

Leto drove through the service entrance and parked behind the maintenance building.

Job and Hannah had just finished a meager breakfast when they heard a car approach. They left the small room and hurried to the window in the main part. They peered through a corner, wondering if their hiding place had been discovered. But he trotted toward the path leading to the edge of the cliff. Once again, he hadn't seen the window they broke to gain access to the building. How long would their luck hold out?

As Leto neared the parking area, he spotted the car he'd seen moments before. It was the same car he'd followed the previous night. He'd tailed her all the way to Bedford, stopping short as she turned into her driveway. He'd given her a moment to get settled inside her house, then searched the mailbox. Myrtle Martin.

The woman standing at the rail had her back to him. From a distance, she appeared to be short and stocky with hair that was predominately gray. She was elderly: beyond seventy and closer to eighty by the look of her. She wouldn't be much of a challenge. His focus was entirely on disposing of the woman who may prove to be a witness. What he failed to do was evaluate the obvious discrepancies between this woman and the woman he saw the previous evening at the ruins.

He needed a final resolution to this unexpected issue in the form of a witness and couldn't have arranged it more perfectly. For at that moment, she was leaning over the rail looking at the ten-foot descent before the vertical drop. She was standing on the balls of her feet which were pressed against a small branch buried halfway into the ground. All he had to do was remove the small branch that supported her position and, at the same time, use the back of her shoes to push forward. She'd slide right over the edge and one problem would be eliminated. The woman who saw him at the ruins the previous evening would disappear. And her death would appear to be a tragic accident due to the misjudgment of an elderly woman.

Two deaths at the same area within days of each other. How would the authorities view this? In his desperate attempt to cover things up, he became irrational. One accidental death and one death by suicide. Couldn't be simpler.

Everything went according to plan. Myrtle Martin let out a short cry as she went over the rail. He didn't stay long enough to watch her fall. Having dispensed with that little problem, he headed along the rail in the direction where the struggle had occurred, leading to the death of his opponent. His head was down, his eyes scanning the area for the remaining pieces of the torn checks in case the wind had carried them this far from the scene.

He'd progressed only a short distance when he heard muted cries coming from the woman he thought he'd disposed of. He should have stayed to make sure it was a clean job. He looked up and that's when he saw her: someone with her chin lowered staring at the ground as she walked slowly in his direction with a camera strap over her shoulder.

He ducked behind a thick brush and watched. With the second cry from Myrtle Martin, the woman raised her head and quickened her pace. He followed her but maintained his cover behind the line of thicket. The woman dropped to her knees and slid forward until her head was over the edge of the cliff. From where he stood, it was impossible to see what took place, but a successful rescue was inconceivable. Although the woman appeared very capable, she was not young either. His lips formed a sliver of a smile. An old woman rescuing an old woman. Perhaps he should intervene before Myrtle Martin had an opportunity to relate how she came to be on the wrong side of the rail. Cautiously, he stepped forward. But as he drew nearer, it became patently obvious that what he thought was inconceivable might actually be accomplished.

Chapter 16

Miss Treadwell heard grunts coming from beyond the rail. "Myrtle!"

"Oh, Cynthia," Myrtle whispered. "I don't know what happened, but I need help."

A large root prevented her neighbor from slipping over the precipice. She gripped a smaller root two feet above where she sat. If she stood, Miss Treadwell could hoist her over the edge. Yet Myrtle's strength was rapidly waning.

Miss Treadwell slid forward with her head hanging over the edge. "I'm going to lower the strap to my camera. Grab hold of it, but you'll have to take one hand off the root to do it. Do you think you can manage it?"

"I'm not sure. I'll try," Myrtle said in a wispy voice.

Taking a firm grasp of the straps where they joined the camera, she extended her arms with the strap dangling within reach of Myrtle's hands. "Take hold one hand at a time."

Myrtle was emotionally attached to the only thing that kept her from falling over the edge to her death. She closed her eyes momentarily and prepared for the worst. Letting go of her left hand, she tried to grasp the strap but failed.

"I know you've reached your absolute limit but try again."

With one triumphant move, Myrtle grabbed the camera strap with one hand.

"Keep your other hand on the root until we make sure I can pull you up here."

"I have enormous faith in you, Cynthia. You're the miracle worker in our neighborhood."

Miss Treadwell felt encouraged, though the fear of failure, resulting in the death of her neighbor, nearly paralyzed her. She pulled while Myrtle used her remaining strength to grip the strap. In a surprisingly short period of time, Myrtle was resting on the ground beside her.

"Are you all right?" Miss Treadwell whispered, noting the scrapes and onset of bruises.

"I think so. But a little worse for wear I'd say." Myrtle closed her eyes and rested while Miss Treadwell pondered how on earth this could have happened. There were rails in place to ensure the safety of anyone observing the beauty of the valley. How could she have ended up falling over the edge of the cliff?

Myrtle opened her eyes and turned her head. "Thank you, Cynthia. I'm afraid I'd be an item in the Bedford obituary column if not for you." With her neighbor's help, she rose slowly to her feet.

There was no denying the accuracy of Myrtle's statement. All Miss Treadwell could do was press her lips firmly together and nod her head.

She took hold of the other woman's arm as she turned toward the car. But Myrtle had enough remaining strength to pull back. "What is it?"

"I want to show you something before we leave," Myrtle said, stumbling as she led the way to the descent from where she'd fallen. "Look beyond where I was perched on that root. Do you see the broken branches torn off bushes where something, or perhaps somebody, rolled over when it fell?"

Miss Treadwell needed a comfortable chair and a cup of tea rather badly. But her neighbor had faced death squarely in the face. The least she could do was spare her a few moments to explain something. She gazed over the dreaded rail but said nothing as she stared at a duplication of what she'd seen only moments before nearly a half mile from where they stood. She'd been so focused on Myrtle, she failed to see beyond where her neighbor crouched hoping to be rescued before she plummeted to her death.

There were obvious signs of something or someone falling down the ten-foot descent to the path below. But were there signs of a struggle as there had been half a mile away? She stepped back. The grass was definitely tramped down, but the cause of the disturbance rested at the feet of the two women. Well, probably another molehill.

"Cynthia." When Miss Treadwell's eyes rose, she said weakly, "You do see what I mean, don't you?"

"Yes. Someone or something rolled down the first ten feet of the drop-off."

"Rather curious, isn't it?"

"Yes, it is," Miss Treadwell said. What was even more curious was how did Myrtle find herself on the wrong side of the rail? "Myrtle, I'm just wondering. How did you happen to fall over the edge?"

Her neighbor remained thoughtful as she considered the possibilities all the while leaning heavily against the rail. "It's a lovely morning. I stood at the rail overlooking the valley. But then my eyes dropped and I saw something that looked unusual. I wanted to lean over the rail and get a closer look, but I'm a little short," she began softly. "I found a branch buried in the ground a few feet from where I stood. It would lift me up several inches so I could look over the edge."

Cynthia studied the ground surrounding the area where she'd discovered her neighbor. "I don't see the branch."

"Well, it's got to be here somewhere."

The two ladies searched until they found it resting ten feet away, on top of rotting leaves left over from last fall.

"Over there," Myrtle said. Miss Treadwell placed a steadying hand under her neighbor's arm as they made their way to where the branch lay partially hidden among the dead leaves. Myrtle placed one hand on her knee for support, bent over slowly, and picked it up. She rotated it while the women examined it closely. Half of it had been buried in dirt. The other half lay above the surface. "I don't understand. This can't be the one I used."

Miss Treadwell gently took the branch from Myrtle's grasp and placed it in the long, dented area her neighbor had used to balance her feet. It was a perfect fit. Miss Treadwell took a number of photos on both sides of the rail. As she studied the photos on the display panel, she felt a cold chill settle in.

"We've seen enough for one day. I suspect we'd best go home now." And with that, the two ladies made their way to the car, walking side by side with Miss Treadwell's hand giving support to her neighbor. They walked in silence. Miss Treadwell was immersed in her own thoughts and versions of "what if".

She considered the scene half a mile along the pathway where there was evidence of an actual struggle leading up to the edge of the cliff. The broken twigs and branches at the first ten feet of the vertical descent were identical at both sites. The difference between the two areas was the obvious struggle that took place at the one farther down the path. If there had been a struggle at the site where Myrtle fell over the edge, it was obliterated by her effort to rescue her neighbor.

Perhaps what she discovered farther down the pathway was something entirely different. Two animals? Impossible. Animals don't push each other over cliffs. Yet she found it hard going dismissing the fact that the ten-foot vertical descent at both sites looked very much the same. She glanced at her neighbor. And what about that small branch? She believed Myrtle's story about using the buried branch for leverage. Therefore, it had obviously been moved.

After securing her neighbor in the passenger seat, Miss Treadwell made her way around to the driver's side using the car as support. On her way, she gazed at the other car parked nearby. There had been no signs of anyone else since they arrived. The car had been covered with dew, but the ground underneath the car was dry, which meant the car was probably here overnight. Did that have anything to do with the torn piece of the check and uprooted grass?

With hands that were none too steady, she placed the key in the ignition and slowly headed for the narrow lane leading down to Cliff Road. It was then her mind began to theorize and she repeated the question she'd asked moments before, "Myrtle, what do you think happened that you ended up over the edge?"

Myrtle was in an oddly mediative mood. "I'm not sure, Cynthia," she said quietly. "But I think I might have been pushed."

Chapter 17

It took several moments and enormous effort, but finally the two women lay exhausted on the ground a few feet from the rail. Was this woman a complete stranger who happened to hear cries for help, or had the two women come together in Myrtle's car? But there was only one other car besides the one he'd left there the day of the—the accident, so the other woman had to arrive with Myrtle Martin. They rose and, instead of returning to the vehicle, they walked back to the rail and looked over the edge.

His eyes drifted across the uneven grass as he contemplated his failure to permanently resolve the situation and debated on what course of action to take next. But they stopped when they spied the camera lying near the spot where the women had rested. He'd seen the camera the second woman carried but failed to internalize its significance.

From the time he spotted Myrtle Martin until he tipped her over the edge, he saw no evidence of a camera. Had the other woman borrowed the camera from Myrtle Martin, or did it belong to her? What photos had she taken? He thought back to the previous evening and suddenly realized the woman who took the photos was not short and frail-looking like the woman he had tried to dispose of moments earlier. The woman he saw last night was agile.

As he studied the two women, he found it increasingly difficult to reconcile the short, somewhat frail-looking woman with the person at the ruins he'd seen kneeling easily to take photos. She rose just as easily, then made her way quickly to her car and drove at a fairly high rate of speed.

Myrtle Martin was the epitome of a white-knuckled elderly driver who puttered down the street ten miles under the speed limit. Could he have been wrong about the identity of the woman he saw last night at the ruins? His mind drifted back as he visualized her kneeling then standing. Suddenly, he knew he'd been wrong. A woman as short as Myrtle Martin would take less time to kneel because she didn't have nearly as much height. The woman last night was taller.

What about the photos she took? It was dark. Even if she'd taken photos of him, which he doubted, they would be darkened images. Could they be edited to lighten them? He'd find out.

Should he bide his time till the two women left, then continue his search? Of course, the wind may have carried the remaining pieces of the checks away and he was worrying over nothing. In any event, she wouldn't recognize the significance of it. The missing pieces could be anywhere from the place where they stood to somewhere along the cliff or carried by the wind all the way to Muddy Creek.

Undoubtedly, he could overpower both of them, search the area for the remaining remnants, take the camera, and be on his way. But what if they put up such a violent struggle, which they undoubtedly would, that he sustained visible injuries? Questions would be asked. He'd have to create a plausible explanation. In the final analysis, it wasn't worth the risk.

He observed the two women while they studied the area. Myrtle Martin hung onto the arm of the other woman. She had faced death and it was a shock, especially for an elderly person. For a solitary moment, he felt a twinge of guilt. Then he remembered what was at stake.

Who was the taller woman? Currently, she was taking photos. Shots were focused on the ground as well as over the rail. Those shots worried him even more. When he first saw her, she was heading away from the area he had come to search. He had to know what she'd seen and photographed then destroy them if they were incriminating. Without the camera as proof, her claims could be written off as the slightly demented rantings of an elderly woman.

He watched closely as the taller woman grasped Myrtle's arm and led her slowly to the car, then seated her gently in the passenger side. It was she who got into the driver's seat, started the car, and drove away. Another crucial detail arose.

The second woman didn't adjust the seat from the position in which she'd found it. Myrtle Martin would have adjusted the driver's seat as close to the steering wheel as possible. The second woman made no adjustments, which meant she drove the car here. Had he been parked closer when he watched her make the left turn from the ruins to the lane leading up to the cliff, he would have noticed that. Myrtle Martin was short enough that her head was below the headrest, which was why he only saw the driver after the left-hand turn was negotiated out of the ruins.

Without breaking cover, he made his way to his car behind the maintenance building. How did the taller woman figure into this? He tapped his fist on the steering wheel in a state of indecision. Was it possible that the taller woman owned the car and the camera? Was it possible she had only stopped at a friend's house on her way home last night and he mistakenly thought it was Myrtle Martin? There could be no second guessing. He called his partner.

"Hannah? I may have been wrong about something."

"What do you mean you may have been wrong about something?"

"I told you I was going back to the cliff area to search for the torn pieces. I'd nearly reached the ruins when I saw Myrtle Martin's car pulling out of the place where she'd parked last night."

"Did she see you?"

"No."

Hannah paused. "What was she doing there?"

"I don't know, and it doesn't matter. Anyway, she had another woman with her," Leto said, then silence fell as he weighed how much to reveal. "Look, there were a few problems at the cliff but I don't want to discuss that right now. I need you to do something for me."

"Like what?" Hannah said guardedly.

"I want you to check Myrtle Martin's garage for a car that matches the year and make I described. If another car is parked in her garage, you'll need to check the neighbors until you find the car."

"Look inside the neighbors' garages? You can't be serious!"

"The owner of the car is also the owner of the camera. There may be nothing on the camera that will hurt me, but I won't know until I see what she's taken. Okay?"

"What will you do if you find photos that will hurt you?"

Leto chuckled. "What do you think? Destroy them!"

"Okay," Hannah said, then paused. "Why don't you check the garages?"

"You know why I can't," he said.

"All right," Hannah said, her voice a study in resentment. "I'll leave right away."

"No. They just left. Give them thirty minutes to get settled."

Once the call ended, he sat looking through the windshield with unseeing eyes. Slowly they focused and he slipped out of the car and headed to the path leading to the edge of the cliff. When he was out of earshot, he called the same number. "The house is fully supplied, right?"

"You know it is. Why do you ask?" Hannah said.

"Because I'm going to grab the two kids sometime today."

"Where did you find them?" Hannah said, attempting to maintain an even voice.

"There's a maintenance building about a half mile from the cliff edge. I checked the building the day they disappeared. Today, I saw a broken window so I know they're in there."

"You won't hurt them, will you?" Hannah said.

"Of course not. Job won't run away once I have her and he can't overpower me."

As soon as the call was discontinued, Hannah made a phone call. "Aunt Vera?"

"Sue Ellen? Are you all right?"

"I'm all right. But Leto is going to pick them up sometime today."

"Today? How did he find them?" Vera said.

"He saw a broken window in the maintenance building that wasn't broken before."

"What does he plan to do with them?"

"Take them to the house," Sue Ellen said.

Even over the phone, their anxiety was palpable. For Sue Ellen's sake, Vera kept her voice calm and steady. "I think they'll be all right."

"How can you say that?" Sue Ellen said.

"Because Leto can't afford to do anything rash right now. It won't be much longer. Just be careful."

Chapter 18

Job and Hannah stood on either side of a back window inside the maintenance building. The survivor didn't appear to notice the broken window. Had he seen it and just not reacted to it? Should they leave? But where would they go? He'd already circled the building twice the day of the murder. Hopefully he would remain confident that the two weren't inside.

Why did he remain in his car? He was talking to someone. Once the call ended, he gazed through the windshield but appeared unfocused. They waited anxiously until he left the car and headed in the direction of the cliff.

"Why does he keep coming back here?" Hannah said, her voice a testimony to the strain of being trapped in a place with no escape and little food.

Job paced while Hannah remained in her customary spot. "He's looking for something. That's the only reason to return."

"Like what?!"

"He's looking for something he left here."

"You mean the body?"

"No, he knows where the body is. He must have hidden it. Maybe he put the body in his trunk and buried it somewhere," Job said. "No, it could only be one thing. Do you remember the two checks that were torn up and tossed into the air?"

"Of course."

"What if someone found them and read whose name is on them?"

"So that's what he's looking for. It's incriminating evidence," Hannah said.

"Someday someone will come here, for a picnic or to see the ruins, and we'll be rescued."

"That could take weeks!" Hannah said. "We could walk to Bedford. It would take a while, but we could do it. We could wait until dark."

"We tried that last night and didn't make it any farther than the ruins before we saw him and had to turn back," Job said. "If he doesn't find what he's looking for today, he'll be back again. What if he catches us before we reach town?"

"And there's nowhere to hide along that road either."

"Maybe you're right. We'll wait until it's closer to dark. It may be worth the risk. Once he leaves, I doubt if he'll make another trip back here today," Job said. "Unless he's figured out where we are and he's waiting for us to come out."

Miss Treadwell parked the car at the end of Myrtle's sidewalk. Living next door, they always walked back and forth to each other's homes. There had only been a handful of times that she'd parked in this spot in the years she lived next door. Now, it was twice within twenty-four hours.

They made their way slowly into the house. Myrtle insisted she didn't need help making tea, so Miss Treadwell collapsed onto the chair she used the night before.

Myrtle tottered from stove to cupboard to refrigerator, mumbling she was a bit low on milk and tea. Finally, she settled herself in a chair opposite her neighbor. She poured tea and, with a trembling hand, lifted the teacup to her lips. They drank their tea in silence for several moments.

In that silence, Miss Treadwell struggled to come to terms with what Myrtle said as they passed the ruins on their return trip home.

"Myrtle, if you truly think someone pushed you over the rail, you need to speak to the police. If you're hesitant, I'll ask Ralph to stop by and you can discuss it with him."

"Cynthia, I am rarely hesitant to do anything. But at seventy-eight, they'll think I'm just an old lady with an incredible imagination. And a foolish old lady at that. I can just imagine what they'll think. 'Poor old dear leaned too far over the rail and lost her balance. She'd probably be safer in an institution.'" She sat back in her chair, reflecting on her options. "Our first impressions are often accurate, but not always. Best let it go for the present, Cynthia. Let me think about it overnight. I ask you not to discuss this with anyone until I decide how I want to handle it. Agreed?"

"All right, Myrtle. I'll remain silent for the present. I'll check back with you tomorrow." She studied her pale, exhausted neighbor. "I'm driving downtown in a few minutes. I'll stop and pick up tea and milk for you. Anything else?"

Myrtle reached for paper and pencil and made a rather long list to Miss Treadwell's dismay.

Thirty minutes after arriving at Myrtle's house, she pulled out of the driveway and parked in her garage. She sat for a moment sorting through her options. One step at a time, and she knew what that next step must be.

Once inside the house, she flipped through her address book until she found Samantha McKean's number. There were two numbers listed. One was the crime lab where Sam worked as a lab technician. The second was her personal cell phone number. Easing herself onto a living room chair, she waited for Sam to answer her cell, mentally crossing her fingers the call wouldn't go to voicemail.

"Hello."

"Sam, I'm so glad you answered the phone."

"Miss Treadwell, how nice to hear from you."

Sam was a busy woman, so Miss Treadwell got right to point. "I took photos in the middle of the night. They're quite dark and I believe they can be edited to lighten them. Am I correct?"

Sam hesitated, wondering why Miss Treadwell was up taking photos in the middle of the night. "You use a camera with a digital card, don't you?"

"Yes, I do." Before any more questions could be asked, she said, "It's nearly eleven o'clock. Would you be free for lunch today? I know it's terribly short notice and you may have other plans, so I completely understand if you can't meet me."

"I'd be delighted to meet you for lunch."

"Teddy's Café across from the police station? That's only a few minutes from the lab."

"Yes, that would be fine."

"Shall we say twelve o'clock then?"

"Twelve o'clock. I look forward to it." Sam sat bewildered by the fact that Ralph's mother wanted to meet her for lunch. Miss Treadwell was not a frivolous person given to wasting someone's time with casual gossip. She'd come to know her rather well through the autumn months the previous year when the older woman claimed she found a dead body beside Muddy Creek. She may be an older woman, but she was far from wilting on the vine. Editing photos to increase viewing capability was something she routinely did. But why had Miss Treadwell taken photos in the middle of the night? And why ask her rather than take them to the camera shop?

Chapter 19

A charming fence divided Miss Treadwell's property from the small park located behind her house. Myrtle admired the fence and extended it through the back of her property as well. Before the year was out, every house on the entire block boasted an identical fence. Anyone who chose could slip over the line of fences into someone's backyard. But people in Bedford respected each other's property. The fence was merely a friendly reminder of where the park's property ended and the backyards began.

After Hannah received the phone call, she drove to the park and appeared to wander aimlessly through the trees. She'd driven past Myrtle Martin's house and counted how many houses it was to the end of the block. So, when she reached her portion of the fence, she stopped, knelt on one knee, and appeared to tie one of her running shoes. Her eyes scanned the empty park. It was still morning, children were in school, and the park was conveniently empty.

She studied the backdoor and windows of Myrtle Martin's house before moving farther down the fence line where the garage blocked any view from the house. She hopped over the fence and moved quickly to the garage window. Her heart sank. The car inside the garage didn't come close to matching the description she'd been given.

Quietly slipping back over the fence, she studied the houses up and down the block, finally settling on the nearest neighbor. Peering through the neighbor's garage window, she confirmed Leto's suspicions. He initially made a serious error because the car did not belong to Myrtle Martin. It belonged to her neighbor. But who was the neighbor? She slipped back over the fence, debating her next move.

At that moment, an older woman walked out the backdoor with her purse under her arm, a camera slung over her shoulder, and a small cooler in her left hand. She walked briskly in the direction of the garage, but her head was turned towards the house, looking at flowers she must have just planted. Breaking into a run, Hannah reached her car, pulled up to the stop sign, and waited. It was a calculated risk. If the woman headed into town, she would drive by the stop sign, and Hannah could follow at a safe distance. If the woman turned in the opposite direction, she'd have to find out her identity some other way.

While she waited, she made a phone call. "Aunt Vera?" she said, trying to maintain an upbeat voice and failing miserably.

"Sue Ellen. How are you holding up?"

"Okay, I guess," Sue Ellen said. "Leto told me to check Myrtle Martin's garage and I did. But the car he saw last night isn't in her garage."

"Okay, go on."

"I looked inside the garage of her neighbor and the car belongs to her. When she came outside, she was carrying a camera. I think she's the woman who took the photos last night. Could you find out who her neighbor is?"

"I don't have to find out," Vera said. "I know who her neighbor is."

"Who is she?"

"Cynthia Treadwell. She's known in the community as Miss Treadwell. Her son is a police officer, Lieutenant Ralph Davies." There was silence while she let Sue Ellen absorb what she said. "Do you intend to tell Leto?"

"Not yet," Sue Ellen said. "I'll wait till I need to use it." Her eyes were focused to the right where Miss Treadwell would appear if she drove into town. Cynthia Treadwell. Aunt Vera seemed so sure that was the neighbor's name. Even so, it would be wise to verify.

Chapter 20

Miss Treadwell drove to the café fifteen minutes early. She wanted to say hello to her eldest son, Teddy, and find a booth in the back where it would be quiet and private.

As she neared the café, she saw a parking spot ahead in front of the police station across the street from where she planned to meet Sam. There was a man about to enter the police station. She knew quite a few people in Bedford but had never seen him before. In any case, he wasn't from Bedford. It wasn't just his outrageously expensive three-piece suit or the kerchief carefully tucked into the breast pocket. No, it was the look of disdain and smugness he wore that set him apart from the other folks in this small town. He wore sunglasses on a day when it was completely unnecessary. What was he doing here?

Jake Prescott pressed through the door as Karl Farrell looked up. Officer Farrell maintained a neutral expression as the New York City lawyer approached his desk. "Anything I can do for you?"

"No," Prescott said. "I came to give you a piece of information."

"Oh, what's that?"

"Have you spoken to the people at the hotel where Grayson is staying?" Prescott asked as if he were questioning a hostile witness in court.

"Not yet," Officer Farrell said briefly. "I've distributed the information and inquiries are being made. The hotel is on the list but we haven't gotten there yet."

Jake Prescott looked over the officer's head and allowed his eyes to drift around the compact room. A far cry from New York. "No one has seen Gray at the hotel. No one can so much as identify him. In fact, the only person who can identify Gray is the desk clerk who checked him into the hotel the evening he arrived." He waited a moment for effect before adding, "And no one knows where the desk clerk is either. Disappeared."

Karl Farrell found that odd but refused to allow any emotion to reach his face. "Did you talk to the manager?"

"Of course I spoke with the manager," Jake Prescott said. "A perfect blank. He had no idea and added no information whatsoever. Hasn't seen Gray. The car he rented isn't in the hotel parking lot. Has no idea where the desk clerk is, and the clerk is the only person who has seen him. I'm thinking of hiring a private detective."

Karl Farrell bit back words he'd like to use. "That's your privilege."

"You're right, Officer. That is my privilege." Jake Prescott left, giving the door a healthy shove.

Karl checked the hotel's phone number, then made the call. "This is Officer Karl Farrell, Bedford Police. Is the manager available?" When the desk clerk indicated he was, Karl asked to speak to him.

"Officer Farrell," the manager said. "I suppose you're calling about this Grayson Matthews situation."

"Yes, I am. What can you tell me about it?"

"Well, not much I'm afraid. Mr. Matthews arrived rather late. No guests were in the lobby and only one person was at the Reservation Desk. His room was definitely used. Bed slept in. Damp towels hanging over the rack. Newspaper read and tossed on the floor. The sort of thing that indicates someone was there overnight."

"Is the car he rented in your parking lot?"

"No. We always keep a record of what car the guest has parked outside. There's no car matching that description in our parking lot."

"I understand your desk clerk disappeared."

"I have no idea what happened. Good employee. Very reliable. Been with me about a month, I'd say. Always on time. Good worker. Good with the guests. To tell you the truth, I'm beginning to worry."

"I can understand that," Karl said. "I'm curious. When the clerk went missing, why didn't you report a missing person?"

"Well," the manager sighed. "I didn't want to get the kid in trouble. Might be a case of just taking off for a while and being back in a day or two. Now, I'm not so sure. Worried something may have happened." Karl heard him murmur to someone who had stepped into his office. "Look, Officer, I'll have to call you back. I am worried and want to know what's happened, but there's a guest putting up a rather impressive fuss and I need to take care of it."

"I understand. Thanks for the information. Someone will check back with you later." Karl Farrell's hand rested on the phone as he pondered the disappearance of two people. Had Grayson Matthews and the hotel desk clerk disappeared at the same time? If they had, was it a coincidence?

Chapter 21

By the time Miss Treadwell reached the space that was open seconds ago, someone else had snagged it. Sighing, she drove around the corner and parked, then made her way through the door of the café. Her eyes scanned the café and came to rest on one of her boys.

Teddy, owner of the café, was the eldest of three she had raised at the group home for boys. The year before Teddy was to be cast out by the system, she bought a house on the outskirts of Bedford and took Teddy, Ralph, and Bobby with her. Teddy and Ralph remained in Bedford. But Bobby had relocated to the west coast.

Feeling someone's eyes on him, Teddy turned, his eyes smiling. He approached and kissed her cheek. "Mom. You're never here this time of day. You okay?"

"Yes, dear," she said, placing her hand on his arm. "I'm meeting Samantha McKean for lunch."

"Sam? Is Sam all right."

"She's fine. It's just that I'm having a little problem with some photos I took and I'm hoping she can help me."

A look of concern crept onto Teddy's face as he glanced at the camera hanging over her shoulder. She was probably the worst liar in Bedford County. As always, she appeared very much in control of herself, but her eyes were troubled and signs of deep fatigue lined her face. "Are you all right, Mom?" he said softly.

Miss Treadwell smiled. There was no pretending around Teddy. "I'm fine, dear. Just being a little silly."

About what, Teddy nearly said, but decided to drop the subject, hoping he'd find out tonight at dinner. "Where do you want sit?"

Miss Treadwell made an unconvincing performance of looking around the room till her eyes rested upon the last booth at the back of the room. "That should be fine."

"It's all yours." Teddy grabbed two menus as he passed the counter, placed them on the table, and headed for the door to greet the next customer.

The young woman was unknown to Teddy. A stranger in Bedford. A stranger is always a curiosity in a small town. She was several inches shorter than Teddy's five-feet-ten-inch height, slender, very young. The hair that could be seen under her beret was a light brown.

He asked if someone would be joining her. No, she was alone. Did she have a seating preference? She also made a pretext of looking around the room, then made her choice. Teddy led her to the seat on the opposite side of the aisle from where his mother sat.

Miss Treadwell opened the display panel and clicked through all the images she'd taken that morning on the clifftop until she reached the photos she'd take in the middle of the night.

They were so dark it was nearly impossible to see what was taking place. The photos of the car were barely discernable against the darkness of the night. The same could be said of the woman in different stages of leaving and returning to the car. They were barely distinguishable from the black background except when she passed in front of the white siding. Those images were marginally better. She could make out the frames where she fell, sat for a time then slowly rose and made her way to the car.

Would Sam be able to edit the images enough to make sense of them? Clicking beyond the photos she took in the middle of the night; she came to the three images of the man at the ruins and unconsciously shivered. She looked up as Sam slid onto the seat opposite hers. "Sam, how lovely to see you."

"It's nice to see you too, Miss Treadwell," Sam said, glancing at the camera. "I see you brought it with you."

"Oh, yes. My camera and I are rarely separated," she said, smiling.

Before looking at the photos, Sam asked an obvious question. "I hope I'm not being intrusive, Miss Treadwell. But I'm very curious to know why you were up taking photos in the middle of the night."

Where to start? At the ruins where she spotted a man who followed her in her car. At least it seemed the man she photographed was the driver of the car. Or would it be better to limit the explanation to last night? Perhaps last night would be less complicated.

"It was one of those dreadfully restless nights, so I was half awake when a car light shone into my bedroom. It was three o'clock," she said with a look somewhere between indignant and concerned. "Someone pulled into Myrtle's driveway. She's the neighbor you met last fall when you stayed with me for a few days."

"Yes, I remember Myrtle Martin very well," Sam said. "I can see why that would be unsettling. Do you think they were lost? Did they pull into the driveway and back out again?"

"That's just it. They didn't leave right away." Miss Treadwell leaned forward. "They pulled all the way up to the sidewalk. A woman jumped out of the car, ran around to the back of the house only to reappear a moment later. After that, the car backed out of the driveway. I thought they were leaving. I say 'they' because the woman sat on the passenger side. But they didn't leave right away. The driver parked for a short time in between streetlights, so it was rather dark, as you'll see in the photos."

Placing the camera into Sam's waiting hands, Miss Treadwell said, "You'll see which ones I'm referring to, Sam." Having delivered her speech, lack of sleep and the tensions and fears of the past eighteen hours caught up with Miss Treadwell. She leaned her head back and closed her eyes.

Sam opened the display panel and clicked through the photos taken that morning. The long-range, high-elevation photos of Muddy Creek surely placed the location on the cliff above the ruins. She'd hiked in that very spot a number of times. She recognized images of trampled down grass. But why would an experienced photographer waste time shooting photos of something as unappealing as grass? If there were only one or two photos, she could chalk it up to pressing the shutter button by accident. But there were at least half a dozen of them. Beyond the photos of trampled-down grass were images that appeared to be tak-

114

en over the railing. And there were photos of a torn piece from a check.

She clicked through those photos, then slowed down as she saw the darkened images. They were vague and undefined. Hopefully she could edit them to the degree necessary to identify what was happening.

Not knowing when those photos ended, she clicked beyond them. These photos were taken at the ruins just below the cliff and were dated the previous evening. But the first three photos differed from the others, which consisted of buildings in various stages of deterioration.

Those three images were of a man. In the first one, he was rising from the step and appeared to be staring directly into the camera. It was a bit blurry. Miss Treadwell must have moved at just that second. The second photo was an interim shot because he started to turn his head toward the camera. The third one was of his profile.

But that was the reverse order from the order in which they'd been taken. The first photo would be the profile, then his head turning toward her. The last photo in the sequence captured him rising from the steps, looking directly at the camera. He appeared to be heading in Miss Treadwell's direction. Viewing the sequence in this manner was unsettling because the third photo had a rather menacing look about it. Was the look menacing or desperate? As a crime lab technician, Sam wasn't given to premature conclusions. But as she closed the display panel, a rare ominous feeling overtook her which had no basis for reality. Or had it?

While Sam reviewed the implications of the photos, her peripheral vision caught someone staring in their direction. She placed the camera on the table and lifted the menu just below her eye level. Yes, the young woman across the aisle was staring at them intently. Sam allowed her eyes to lift for a fraction of a second and realized the woman wasn't focused on them. Her focus was aimed at the camera. But why?

Chapter 22

When Miss Treadwell awoke, Sam fought the temptation to quiz her about the three photos of the man at the ruins. The purpose of this lunch was to discuss the shots she'd taken at three o'clock in the morning, and she stuck to it.

"I see what you mean. In the middle of the night, the photos are naturally dark. The objects almost blend in with their surroundings, but they're still visible, just difficult to interpret. Let me see what I can do at the lab. I should be able to edit the objects so we have a better idea of what's happening."

"I don't want you to feel pressured, Sam. But how long do you think it will take to do that?"

"Not long. If you follow me back to the lab after lunch, I'll do it while you wait."

"Thank you so much, Sam. That's very thoughtful of you." Miss Treadwell felt the tightness of her muscles loosen a trifle. If peace didn't completely envelope her, she felt a certain amount of the burden lift from her shoulders. Perhaps it was sharing one of the mysteries with someone else. But other mysteries remained in the shadow.

As she relaxed, Sam studied her. She'd gotten to know Ralph's mother fairly well last fall when the older woman claimed to have discovered a dead body at Muddy Creek. She was steadfast and resilient, not given to idle chatter or dramatization. At that moment, Miss Treadwell was deeply worried. Was the focus of her worry the three o'clock incident? Of course, that would be a great concern to anyone. Or was there something else she wasn't revealing? If there was, what could it be to create that drawn expression? Did it have anything to do with the three photos of the man at the ruins she'd taken the previous evening?

Miss Treadwell covered a yawn, smiled, and said, "I'm afraid I didn't get much sleep last night. Do you know what you want to order?"

Their eyes swept through the menu and they ordered as soon as Teddy arrived. The café was short-staffed that day, which placed him in the position of wearing several hats.

Having taken their order, Teddy crossed the aisle and took the young woman's order.

"Just coffee?" Teddy said. Rarely did someone order only coffee this time of day.

"Just coffee." She glanced across the aisle, then back at Teddy. "Can you bring the check with the coffee?"

"Sure, I'll bring the check with your coffee."

Before the server left, Hannah said, "I know I've met the woman in the booth across the aisle, but I can't remember her name."

"Which one?" Teddy said, taking a closer look at the young woman.

She wore a beret which not only covered part of her hair but slid down hiding the side of her face as well.

"The older lady."

Teddy looked at his mother, then turned back. He hesitated, but before the young woman could detect his hesitation, he said, "Her name is Cynthia Treadwell."

"Oh, yes," she said. "Cynthia Treadwell." That confirmed what Vera had told her. When the server was out of sight, Hannah dropped her head slightly as if to read a pamphlet she kept in her purse for just that purpose. But her eyes were focused on Myrtle Martin's neighbor. Her gaze was so focused, she was unaware that she was also under subtle scrutiny by the woman sitting across from Miss Treadwell.

Teddy left to brew the woman's coffee. But as he rounded the corner of the counter, a low level of anxiety rose within him. Sooner or later, most people in Bedford entered his café. He thought he knew everyone his mother knew. The fact that he'd never seen a woman who claimed to know his mother wasn't the issue. It was that tone of voice that spoke of familiarity with someone but a moment of forgetfulness. He couldn't describe or account for this feeling that something was off. And it centered on the young woman he'd just waited on.

Hannah made her move when she saw the server take their plates and leave the check. She left the café, got in her car, and waited. Within minutes, the two women walked through the door and got into separate cars. The younger woman led the way, followed by the older woman, Cynthia Treadwell. Hannah allowed them a half-block then fell in behind them.

As they left the café, Sam walked to her car with her head straight ahead while her eyes searched the parked cars. When she spotted the young woman waiting in a car across the street, her steps slowed considerably. Pulling herself together, she resumed her pace, got in her car, and waited for Miss Treadwell to pull up behind. Her eyes rotated between the windshield and the rear-view mirror. For the initial two minutes, only Miss Treadwell's car was visible.

In a moment of lost focus, Miss Treadwell drifted to the side and Sam spotted the car. Why was the woman following them? She pulled into the crime lab's parking lot and waited while Miss Treadwell parked beside her. Once again, her head remained straight as her peripheral vision caught sight of the young woman's car.

Sam opened the car door for Miss Treadwell, which gave her the opportunity to pivot her body to the street. The car that appeared to be following them drove past the lab and kept on going. It had been nothing more than a coincidence.

Once inside the building, Sam took the digital card out of the camera and walked through a door behind a counter. She slid the digital card into the card reader, then edited each dark photo on the computer screen until the contrast was great enough to see what the individual photos held. One photo depicted the woman in different stages of falling, then rising again and moving forward at a slower rate. The slower rate was evident by the shorter steps. The woman must be in pain for she grasped her injured hand.

There was one photo that stood out from the others Miss Treadwell had taken at three o'clock in the morning. She enlarged it on the screen then enlarged a certain area. Sitting back in her chair, disturbing thoughts surfaced. It was those distressing thoughts that pressed Sam to click farther back to view other photos.

She clicked back until she reached the three images of the man sitting on the steps at the ruins. There was something about this man that dredged up a vague memory, but the first two photos were of his profile, so it was difficult to know if he was someone she knew. Perhaps he only reminded her of someone. The third photo of the man turning toward the camera was a bit blurred, making identification even more difficult.

Was she out of line editing those three photos in addition to the ones Miss Treadwell had requested? Her experience in the crime lab justified it, knowing it may be important at some point if something hidden within her conscious mind eventually surfaced. Was there a remote possibility that all these photos had anything to do with the woman following them?

She edited the three images of the man at the ruins and printed them with the other photos she'd edited for Miss Treadwell. She thought for a moment, then printed two copies, one for Miss Treadwell and one for herself. Should she include the three photos of the man with the others? Tapping the three photos on the edge of the desk, she decided against it and slid them inside the top drawer.

Miss Treadwell wandered around the room, glanced at her watch, picked up magazines and put them down again. Her thoughts shifted from the photos she'd taken a few hours ago at the top of the cliff to the three-o'clock prowlers she'd seen that morning, and finally to the man she photographed at the ruins the evening before.

A thought occurred to her. When she left the ruins the previous evening, she had been on the road for a few miles before she saw car lights in her rear-view mirror. So, if the man she photographed was the one following her, he'd parked his car some distance from where he sat; otherwise he would have caught up to her in a very short period of time.

Or could someone else have been following her?

Sighing rather heavily, she very much worried she was falling into the same trap as Myrtle Martin in that she'd be considered an elderly woman given to frivolous whims of fancy. She cast those thoughts aside when the lab door opened.

Four-by-six-inch photos of the shots she took in the middle of the night were placed on the counter facing Miss Treadwell. "This is as light as I can make them and still maintain clarity." Sam remained silent as the older woman slowly viewed each of the twelve photos.

"Did you see the photo of the woman against the white siding? It's the one where she's about to walk around the corner to the back of the house."

Sam nodded, but her eyes remained on the photos. The power of suggestion is very strong, and she didn't want to influence her.

Miss Treadwell studied the photo again. "It looks like…."

Sam waited. "Looks like what?"

"It looks like she's carrying an object. I'm not quite sure what it is, but it looks like a gun."

Chapter 23

The lunch crowd was heavy that day, but Teddy's subconscious mind wouldn't rest. His mother was a woman of rather strict routine. She'd broken her routine today and it was unsettling. More than that was the look of utter fatigue and restraint in her eyes, as if she were struggling with something and not quite ready to reveal what it was. If the young woman had quizzed him about anyone else, he would have forgotten the incident in seconds. But it was his mother who had loved him, given him a home when he had nowhere to go, and loaned him the money to open the café.

When there was a break, Teddy walked into his office, closed the door, and made a phone call. "Ralph?"

"Teddy, how are things going?" Ralph said.

"Well, I don't know, Ralph. You'll probably think I've become an alarmist."

Having followed up on unfinished business, Ralph was driving back to Bedford. "What's happened?"

"Mom was here for lunch. She's never here for lunch. Doesn't like the crowd."

"I know. Mom doesn't like crowds."

"She called Sam to meet her here. I mean, that's nice," Teddy said, trying to tamp down this feeling of overreacting to a simple luncheon engagement. "Mom had her camera with her. She talked to Sam for a while then gave her the camera. Evidently she wanted Sam to see something."

Ralph couldn't put his finger on it, but it was so out of sync with what their mother did. "I'm not sure what to make of it either. It may be nothing. We don't know yet."

"I get it, but here's the thing, Ralph." At this point, Teddy felt like someone spying in an intrusive sort of way. "When Sam looked through the images on the display panel, her expression grew, how shall I say, sober toward the end. She didn't have any particular expression on her face up to that point. I don't know what to make of it." There was hesitation born of the worry he was about to impart. "There was a young woman who came in right after Mom did. She ordered coffee for lunch, which is unusual, but that's not what worries me."

"Go on."

"She asked who Mom was. Said she thought she recognized her but didn't remember her name. She didn't ask about Sam, just who Mom was."

Ralph visualized the scene. As an experienced police officer, he didn't allow himself to jump to conclusions. "Any idea who the young woman was? Ever seen her before?"

"Never seen her before. No idea who she is."

"Describe her to me."

"Well, she was three or four inches shorter than I am, so about five feet six or seven. Slender, light brown hair, dressed in jeans and a polo shirt. Wore a beret which hid part of her hair and face. Young. Maybe twenty."

In spite of the rather odd circumstances, Ralph smiled. Teddy noticed and remembered everything. "Okay. I hear you, Teddy. Let's hope Mom brings this up tonight. It's none of our business, but we want to make sure nothing's wrong. And I don't know what to think about the young woman. If she comes in again, let me know. If I'm at the station, I'll walk across the street and take a look. See if I recognize her."

"Okay. Thanks, Ralph."

Ralph normally drove with both hands on the wheel. As soon as he turned onto the main road leading into Bedford, he placed his elbow on the window ledge, and rubbed his chin.

His mind drifted back to the knock on the door when he was five years old. His babysitter answered the door. Two police officers stood there and asked the young girl to take the little boy to another room to play. Instead of staying in the playroom, he crept back to the side of the door and listened. His parents had been killed in a car accident. When he heard those words, his ears refused to hear anymore.

Later, someone picked him up and drove an hour away to the Group Home For Boys. He had vague memories of that first month. Cynthia Treadwell rocked him every day for an hour, humming so the sound reverberated from her chest to his ear. By the end of that month, she was his mother. For the next eleven years, he shared a room with Teddy and Bobby.

When he was sixteen, his mother bought a house large enough for the three boys and herself. They moved to Bedford and that became their home.

His mind shifted from his mother to Sam and he gave her a quick call. "Sam?" He heard the smile in her voice, which reduced some of the tension he felt a moment ago.

"Hi. Are you on your way back to Bedford?"

"Just turned onto the main road. Be at my desk in twenty minutes," he said. "How's your day been?"

"Fine," Sam said tentatively. "Actually, I met your mother at Teddy's Café for lunch. She asked me to edit some photos she took late at night. I did that and she's already left. But I'm a little uncomfortable. Some odd things have happened. Would you have a few minutes to stop by the lab? I'd really like to discuss them with you."

'Photos she took late at night'? 'Some odd things have happened'? The tension returned, only with greater intensity this time. He and Sam understood each other very well. She was not easily distressed over insignificant events. If something odd happened, he'd make time to stop and discuss it. "I hear you, Sam. I'll be at the lab in a few minutes."

"Good," Sam said. "Why don't you use the back entrance. If the staff room is free, we'll talk in there."

"Okay. See you in a few minutes." To the best of his knowledge, after the Muddy Creek case was resolved, Sam and his mother never met for lunch. She often joined them for Wednesday night dinners, but never lunch as far as he knew. Was it just to have photos edited, or was there something more than that?

The unspoken question was, why ask Sam to edit the photos rather than the Bedford Camera Shop? His mother knew the owner quite well. What photos had she taken that she didn't want him to see?

He met his mother when he was five years old. Even then she was an amateur photographer. Would she take photos when it was so dark the images needed to be edited solely for that purpose? What were the circumstances that forced her to take them? Again, it just didn't feel right. When something doesn't feel right, it usually isn't.

Ralph stretched his shoulders. It had been a tiring, stressful day and it was only two o'clock.

His mind reverted to the young woman who pretended to know his mother. That didn't feel right either. Might be nothing. Hoped it was nothing.

Chapter 24

Ralph drove to the back of the lab where Sam was waiting for him. She opened the door and he stepped through. Her face was drawn and he slipped his arms around her and drew her close.

"I don't want to worry you, Ralph," Sam said softly.

Ralph smiled. "My job is to worry."

They sat across from each other at a table. Ralph waited while Sam collected her thoughts. The police mantra was "start at the beginning," and so she did.

"Your mother called me about eleven o'clock asking me to join her for lunch at Teddy's Café around noon. She's never done that before, so I knew it wasn't just a casual invitation. She brought her camera with her." Sam stopped for a moment. "This isn't idle gossip, Ralph. You know that."

"I know. Something's happened or you wouldn't have asked me to stop by."

Sam offered a weak smile and continued. "A car pulled into Myrtle Martin's driveway at three in the morning. A woman ran to the back of the house, returned a few minutes later, and the car backed out again. But it didn't leave. It parked at the side of the street for a short time."

Ralph waited. He knew this was just the beginning.

"Your mother took quite a few photos. They were dark and needed to be edited. She got very little sleep last night, so while I was looking at the display panel, she leaned back and took a nap." Sam took a breath, pulling the next part into a cohesive thought. "Sometimes you can feel someone's eyes on you. There was a young woman sitting directly across the aisle from us. I saw her staring in our direction out of the corner of my eye. But she wasn't looking at either of us. She was staring at the camera. We were nearly finished when she left. I confess I was relieved. Yet, when I walked outside the café, I saw her waiting in her car on the other side of the street."

"Was she waiting for you?"

"I thought so at the time. Now, I'm not so sure," Sam said. "I checked in my rear-view mirror. Your mother's car was directly behind me because she was following me to the lab. But I also saw that woman's car behind her. Just fleeting glances when your mother's car drifted to the side. Once we reached the parking lot and got out of our cars, I saw her approach, but she kept on going." Sam stopped for a moment and studied Ralph's face.

The inner tension from Teddy's call grew as Sam's story unfolded. Yet his face remained interested, focused, but neutral. "There's more."

"Yes, there's more. At the café, I saw photos she'd taken that unnerved me." Sam withdrew photos from an envelope she'd edited for

Miss Treadwell, including the photos taken at three thirty in the morning and the three photos of the man at the ruins. She placed them in front of Ralph, separating the three at the ruins from the others. "Your mother took these three last night." Sam "The display panel indicated they were taken around seven o'clock."

Ralph studied all of them, then focused on the three taken at the ruins. Sam had placed them in the order in which they were taken. He saw the photo of the man's profile ending with the man rising out of his seat and staring into the camera. He studied the face. Even with editing, it was still difficult to know who it might be. The last photo was blurry and the others were profile photos. Mom must have been unnerved and moved the camera slightly. That fact jarred him as much as anything else had so far. He continued to study the photos until he knew his face was under control. He looked up and knew instantly Sam wasn't finished, so, once more, he waited.

"I walked your mother to her car, but as I returned to the lab, I saw the tail end of the same car heading in the same direction as your mother. At least I think it was the same car. I wrote down the description of the car I saw at the café," Sam said, then slid a small sheet of paper across the table with the details on it and held one hand while he read the note with the other. "It may be nothing more than a coincidence. I ran back inside to get my keys and follow them…."

Ralph squeezed her hand. "By that time they would have been out of sight." He reached for his phone and tried to call his mother. No answer.

"I've tried calling her, too. Several times."

"When did Mom leave?"

"No more than two minutes before you called me."

Ralph checked his phone. He'd called Sam eighteen minutes ago. Mom had time to drive home if she went there directly. He tried calling her land phone. Then he tried again, and a third time.

Ralph studied the note and slipped it inside his shirt pocket. For several moments, they sat quietly holding hands across the table as he internalized everything Sam had said and considered how to respond to it. "You did well to tell me. Mom is expecting Teddy and me for dinner tonight. I'm sure she'll discuss everything with us."

Ralph drove the short distance from the crime lab to the station. Was this an extraordinary series of coincidences or something more?

Chapter 25

Ralph's mind was in conflict as he walked through the police station door. Should he put out an alert? Would he do that if the person was anyone but his mother? No, he'd give it more time. "Any messages, Karl?" he said to the officer on duty.

"A few. I placed them on your desk," Karl said, then gave Ralph a several minutes to settle in before filling him in on the visits from Grayson Matthews' lawyer.

Ralph made his way down the hall, hoping Chief Henderson wouldn't call him into his office. He looked through the messages on his desk but his eyes wouldn't focus. Maybe he was tired. Then he noticed a message set aside. Why was it not with the others? Did Karl consider it unimportant, or had it just come in and he tossed it on the desk?

A missing person report had been filed. He recognized the name, Grayson Matthews. Matthews arrived in Bedford a few days ago. No accompanying photo; just a short article in the newspaper about him.

Had the man driven to Bedford County then left? Or had he remained in Bedford County and gone into hiding for whatever reason? It wouldn't be the first time a celebrity or well-known figure went into hiding to get away from the constant scrutiny of the public eye.

Karl tapped on his door then slipped inside. "You saw the missing person report?"

"I did. Grayson Matthews. He drove up here to do some fishing. Now he's reported as missing?"

"Right. His lawyer, Jake Prescott, called and wanted it filed. Arrived by chartered plane. Staying at the same hotel as Matthews. Been here twice already. Apparently Matthews got to his hotel late. No one was around except the desk clerk. When Matthews disappeared, so did the desk clerk. That's what the lawyer said. I called the hotel and the manager verified everything the lawyer told me. Said the car Matthews drove to the hotel isn't in the parking lot. Said the desk clerk had been with him for about a month and was reliable. No idea where the clerk is. There was a problem at the front desk and he had to leave before I could ask any more questions."

"I'll ask Jody to give him a call." Ralph leaned back in his chair as he studied the missing person report with unseeing eyes. "Two people missing from the hotel at the same time," he said softly. "That's odd. Especially when one of them is Grayson Matthews."

"Very odd," Karl said. Having delivered his message, he left to cover the front desk.

Ralph punched in Jody's number. "Jody, you know about Grayson Matthews missing, right?"

"Yes, Karl briefed all of us."

"Karl contacted the hotel manager. He said the only person who saw him the night he arrived was the desk clerk. Now the desk clerk is missing as well. The manager had to hang up before Karl could get any more details. I want you to talk to the hotel manager. Find out where the clerk lives. It doesn't seem logical that the two disappearances are connected, but we need to consider it a possibility. Let me know what you find out."

"Okay, I'll get right on it, Ralph."

"One more thing, Jody. The car Matthews drove to the hotel isn't in the parking lot. The hotel will have a record of the make, model, and license number. Take care of that while you have him on the phone."

"Right. I'll take care of it."

Ralph looked out his window, putting aside the missing person report, and thought of his mother and Sam. The two women he loved breaking a routine. Where was his mother, and was he reading too much into this? He punched in her number, but there was no answer. Was this just a series of events with an odd twist to it, or something more? The topic would come up at dinner that night. He'd ask Teddy to bring it up. Although, he probably wouldn't need to. His brother was a genius at bringing up a subject without appearing to be prying. Returning to his desk, he forced his mind to concentrate on the work at hand.

Hannah waited around the corner from the lab where Cynthia Treadwell's car was parked. The camera went into the lab with the older woman. Even if she'd left the camera in her car, the lab was located in too public a place to snatch it. When she saw the older woman's car pass by she followed her at a distance. Hope died at the next stop when the camera went into the camera shop. It was a shorter wait this time. The older woman reappeared carrying the camera. She walked slowly; her eyes focused on the ground.

Once there was sufficient distance between the cars, Hannah picked up the tail once again. She sighed deeply when the front car turned into a residential area. It was a narrow, tree-lined street. Why did it have to be this street? It was a neighborhood of rowhouses with small windows where neighbors knew each other and were instantly suspicious of strangers. But she already knew that, having been here the previous night.

When the Treadwell woman pulled into Crandall's Corner Market, Hannah parked under the protective covering of overhanging limbs. If she left her camera in the car, an opportunity had just been handed to her.

Chapter 26

Now that the issue of the dark photos had been resolved, Miss Treadwell needed enlargements of the suspicious-looking pictures she'd taken at the top of the cliff that morning. With the enlarged photos, she could evaluate whether or not she needed to discuss her concerns with Ralph that evening.

She sat for a moment outside the camera shop. Exhaustion threatened to derail her plans for the rest of the day. Taking a deep, somewhat shaky breath, she lifted her camera from its cushion on the floor and walked into the shop.

The owner of the shop knew this customer very well. "Afternoon, Miss Treadwell. Got some photos you want printed?"

"Actually, I want about a dozen enlarged this time. Say eight-by-ten." She gave him the digital card out of her camera and the numbers of the photos she wanted enlarged. "How long do you think it will take?"

"As soon as I copy the photos you want to my computer, I'll return your digital card to you," he said. "Should have the enlargements ready for you in an hour."

"They'll be ready in an hour? You are a miracle worker," she said with a smile. Her smile was the reason he dropped everything to make the enlargements in an hour rather than the customary twenty-four hours like everyone else.

Moments later Miss Treadwell headed for Crandall's Corner Market. An hour would give her plenty of time to pick up the items on Myrtle's list.

Parking near the entrance, she walked through the door but the store was empty. Where was everyone? Currently, "everyone" was Mr. Crandall. His assistant, Robbie, was still missing. She'd gather the things on Myrtle's list. Perhaps he'd hear her rattling around and walk through the back door. Ten minutes later, with everything stacked on the counter, she knocked on the back door. Mr. Crandall came through in a rather harried state, apologizing profusely.

He was about five feet eight inches tall, which meant he stood the same height as Miss Treadwell. Height was one of the reasons he'd hired Robbie. Robbie was over six feet tall and could reach items without a ladder.

Mr. Crandall was a slight man, so he didn't weigh but twenty pounds more than she did. Nearly the same age, Miss Treadwell's hair was sprinkled with gray. The little hair Mr. Crandall had was completely gray. He always wore a white shirt to the market. Said it gave the impression of cleanliness.

"Oh, Miss Treadwell. Didn't hear you walk through the door. Sorry to keep you waiting," he said, hurrying along the aisle to the cash register at the front.

"That's all right. Any news about Robbie?"

"Still missing," Mr. Crandall said as he rang up the first item. "Hasn't been here for three days now! No idea where he is. Left at quitting time, same as always. Said he'd see me the next morning like he always does. He's worked for me long enough that I'm sure he'd call if something was wrong and he couldn't come to work. There's a reason he hasn't called and that's what worries me."

"Yes, I'd be very concerned, too," Miss Treadwell said sympathetically.

"After I closed the store the first day he didn't show up, I walked over to his place. Only lives a couple of blocks from here. Don't believe I mentioned that yesterday."

"No, I don't think you did."

"Knocked on the door. I could see Helen was worried, too. That's his landlady."

"Yes, you mentioned Helen was his landlady."

"Helen had no idea where Robbie was either." Mr. Crandall leaned sideways against the counter. "Helen lives downstairs, you see. Robbie has the second floor to himself. Now, I know his landlady because she comes in here every Thursday to buy what she needs. Well, used to anyway." He turned to Miss Treadwell as a thought occurred to him. "You probably know Helen. Takes yoga with your neighbor, Myrtle Martin."

"Oh, yes, Myrtle has mentioned Helen several times," Miss Treadwell said.

"I figured you knew Helen. Comes here on Thursday," he repeated.

"Yes, I do understand," she said briefly, wondering what the end of the story would reveal.

"Paid his rent on time and didn't mess up his place, so he was a good tenant. She was about two minutes away from calling the police to report a missing person," he said as he rang up her merchandise.

"Do you know if she called?"

"I stopped by last night and she hadn't called. Haven't talked to her today." He stroked his chin a moment, then added, "Might be I'll just close up the store and run down to the police station. I know Jody pretty well. She's one of the officers," he said, then shook his head. "Plumb forgot. One of your boys is a police officer down there, right? You probably know Jody."

"Yes, Ralph Davies," Miss Treadwell said. "And I do know Jody. She's a lovely person."

"Yep, regular customer. Comes here couple of times a week. Lives down the street," he said, quite forgetting he'd mentioned this before. "Lives half a block from where Robbie lives. Wonder if she knows anything about him. I'll give her a call later and ask her about him. I could probably report Robbie as a missing person over the phone. What do you think?"

"Yes, I suspect Jody would do that. I think that's a very good idea. Robbie is a nice young man. I'd hate to think something's happened to him." She watched as he bagged everything, then rearranged them twice. She had a few minutes until her prints were ready. "Would it help if I stopped by Robbie's apartment and had a look around?"

Relief flooded Mr. Crandall's face. "Would you do that? He doesn't have anybody in this world to look after him. Parents both dead. Never talks about it. I've sorta taken him under my wing if you know what I mean. Truth is, I've become very attached to the boy." He wiped his hands on his long, white apron and reached for the phone. "Helen? Has Robbie come back by any chance? I see. Well, look. Miss Treadwell's here. She's Myrtle Martin's neighbor. Oh, you know who she is? I figured you might with you taking yoga and all. I'd sure be grateful if you'd let her take a look through Robbie's apartment. Her son's a police officer. Oh, you know that, too. Well, she sorta knows about things like that since her son's on the police force."

Miss Treadwell wondered just what Myrtle had said about her during yoga class. And what made him assume she knew about things like that because Ralph was on the police force.

He put his hand over the phone. "Helen wants to know if you'll be there shortly." When she nodded her head, he said, "She'll be right there, Helen."

Myrtle had given her cash to pay for her grocery items. Mr. Crandall handed her a few dollar bills and was about to follow with coins when he drew back.

"Is something wrong?" Miss Treadwell said as he flipped the coin over and checked the back of it.

"I didn't catch this one earlier. Might be worth some money," he said, placing it in a cup located on a shelf behind the counter and offering another coin out of the register.

"You're a coin collector."

"Oh, yes. Collected coins for years. Thought it would be a good hobby for Robbie, so I started teaching him what to look for. He's gotten pretty good at it. Good investment for him."

"Do you get many coins worth collecting in the course of a day?"

"Once a week is more like it. I don't cheat anyone, you understand," Mr. Crandall hastened to assure. "I always tell'em what they're giving away. Most people don't care about it. I keep them in that cup behind me now that Robbie is interested. He looks for them and asks the same question. I've given him a dozen coins to start his own collection. Bought him a coin storage box and a little book to go with it." He dropped his eyes. "He's a good kid. I miss him."

Miss Treadwell reached across the counter and placed her hand on his arm. "He'll turn up. I feel certain of that."

Chapter 27

Hannah sat in her car as people walked by the corner market. Twice, the coast was clear and she got out of her car only to slip back inside again when someone came around the corner. She tapped her fingertips on the bottom of the steering wheel as she waited. She pulled down the visor and swung it around to the side window. It hid part of her face from anyone walking past her car on the sidewalk. Small towns were notoriously curious about outsiders. But whenever there was a break in the sidewalk traffic, a curtain fluttered at a window. It was useless. There was no way to determine how long the Treadwell woman would be in the corner market. This was rapidly becoming a waste of time. Digging in her purse, she grabbed a small envelope with a key inside, then wrote a note.

"Aunt Vera, I've been trying to take Miss Treadwell's camera for the past hour. She's parked at the corner market and it's impossible to get it. I'm afraid if Leto gets it before I do, he'll destroy the photos. Here's the key to the house. You may need it at some point. Love, Sue Ellen"

After writing the note and placing it inside the envelope, she slipped out of her car, walked across the street, and shoved the envelope through the mail slot. No one would question dropping off a note. Returning to her car, she drove slowly out of town.

If all else failed, she'd wait till dark when Miss Treadwell was at home asleep. But breaking into someone's house was always a huge risk. She'd done that very thing the previous night two blocks down the street from where her car had been parked. The difference was she had a key to gain entrance. There were no broken windows. If luck was with her, she could carry it off again tonight, key or no key. But luck had a way of running out at the most inconvenient times.

After placing certain items in the cooler she'd brought along for just that purpose, Miss Treadwell drove the short distance to the house where Robbie had lived until three days ago.

Helen met her at the door, sizing up the woman she'd heard about at yoga class. Her lined face was a study in a woman's struggle to survive a difficult life. She wore a faded print housedress popular thirty years earlier. It hung on her as though she'd lost considerable weight or had inherited it from someone who weighed twenty pounds more than she did. A short woman, about Myrtle Martin's height, she tilted her head as she gazed up at the woman in her doorway.

Without a hint of the customary preliminaries, Helen said, "So, you live next door to Myrtle."

Miss Treadwell smiled as brightly as anyone who has been wrung through the gossip wringer was capable. "Yes, Myrtle and I have been neighbors for a number of years."

"She said you don't see much of that son of yours who moved out west."

Miss Treadwell's smile lost some of its glitter. "Not as much as I'd like," she said, then changed the subject. "Mr. Crandall mentioned that Robbie lives in your house?"

"He has the upstairs to himself. I rent it furnished. He only brought one big suitcase and a box of stuff. Didn't have much."

"And you haven't seen or heard from him for the past three days?"

Helen's eyes slid away for a second. "Well, no, not exactly," she said guardedly.

Before Miss Treadwell could question her further, Helen turned on her heel and led the way down the narrow hall to the kitchen, then up the equally narrow stairway which creaked with every step. "There would be no doubt when Robbie came and went," she said, opening the door for information she knew was being withheld.

"That's right; I hear every sound," Helen said. "I know his footsteps. Heard them often enough. Sorta look forward to hearing them. Guess we all have our own footsteps." She leaned heavily on the rail as they made their way slowly to the top. "I'll unlock his apartment and leave you to it."

Miss Treadwell stood in the middle of a small, sparse, lifeless room. Not a picture or ornament hung anywhere throughout the three rooms and bath. Threadbare, mismatched furniture was carelessly positioned at intervals. Where to start and what to look for? She wandered through the rooms, feeling every bit the snoop she disliked in others.

Opening the bedroom closet door, the contents revealed an orderly young man. Robbie had very little, but what he had was tidy. She was about to close the door when she noticed a photo of a couple pinned to the inside of the door. Easily missed. Why had he placed it here? It was a small black-and-white photo. The couple were middle-aged and dressed in the style of the mid-sixties rather than current. His grandparents perhaps? No doubt they would look vastly different now if they were still alive. It was the only photo she'd seen in the few moments she'd been in the apartment. It had to be significant, yet why did Robbie hide it inside his closet rather than have it framed and placed out in the open?

In the living area, Robbie had a table set up beside the window overlooking the alley in back of the house. Her eyes came to rest on a small box placed to the side. Was that the coin storage box Mr. Crandall mentioned? He said he'd given him a dozen coins, but did a dozen still remain? Opening the box, she counted them. Eleven. If Mr. Crandall had been accurate, one was missing.

There were only a few other objects: two magazines, a few pieces of paper with a pencil lying on top, and a calendar book. Leafing through the calendar she observed the young man led a rather uneventful life. Nearly every page was blank. Suddenly, she stopped and leafed through the previous week again. A page had been torn out. It was the day he went missing. When she pressed the pages down as flat as possible, she saw the tear marks. What had he written that he didn't want anyone to see? Or had someone else torn it out? She leaned back in the chair. But in the process of leaning back, the calendar tilted and a slip of paper floated to the floor.

She leaned to pick it up. It was a small rectangular note torn from Crandall's Corner Market. It must have been a note Robbie wrote while he was at work to remind himself of something. "Teddy's Café, six o'clock." The date written on the paper was the date he disappeared.

Digging her phone out of her purse, she called Teddy. It was the slow time of day and he answered immediately.

"Mom? Everything okay?"

Her son was worried about her, so she kept her voice light and cheerful. "Fine, dear. Myrtle needed a few things so I stopped at the corner market. Robbie works there. Do you know him?"

"Robbie? Sure, I know him."

"Well, he hasn't shown up for work in three days. Mr. Crandall is very worried about him, so asked me to check his apartment to see if I could discover anything that might lead to his disappearance. He plans to call Jody and report Robbie as a missing person. I'm sitting at the table in his apartment right now. There's a note he wrote reminding him to be at your café at six o'clock three nights ago. Do you remember anything about it?"

"Robbie's missing and no one knows where he is?"

"Even his landlady doesn't know his whereabouts. You may be the last person to have seen him."

"Hm. Three nights ago," Teddy murmured. "Oh, yes. Robbie was here. Said he was waiting for someone to join him. Ordered something to drink, but she never showed up so he left."

"He was waiting for a woman?"

"Well, I joked around with him about being stood up. He said something must have happened to change her mind, so that's when I knew he was waiting for a woman."

"'Did he seem upset about it?"

"Upset?" Teddy said as his mind played back the scene. "A little. Anxious more than angry about it. He tapped the spoon on the table. Didn't make much noise, but I noticed it. Stared at the door and the clock a lot. So, yes, I'd say he was worried. I just didn't think about it at the time. I figured it was a first date with her and he was nervous."

"And he left without mentioning who he was waiting for or where he was going afterward?"

"Not a word."

"All right, dear," she said absently. "I'll see you tonight."

"Okay, Mom. Let me know if there's anything I can do to help."

Concerned that Helen was counting the minutes until she reappeared, Miss Treadwell descended the staircase, creaking with every step. But as she rounded the corner into the kitchen, Helen stood waiting for her. She faced the stairway with downcast eyes and fingers clasped in front of her. "Are you all right, Helen?" she said softly.

Helen laughed, but the merriment didn't reach her eyes. "Just being silly," she said. But there was that look on her face that hoped the other woman would press her for an answer, and more importantly, believe her story.

Chapter 28

"I sense there's something you want to talk about," Miss Treadwell said hesitantly.

"Well, I'm just being silly," Helen said again. She turned to the stove where a kettle was about to whistle. "I, uh, I was going to have a cup of tea. I don't suppose you'd like to join me? You probably like coffee. Anyway, you're probably too busy."

"Tea?" Miss Treadwell smiled. "I never turn down the prospect of a cup of tea."

Helen was reclusive. Not accustomed to talking. At yoga, she listened rather than contributed to the gossip. Never entertained guests. "Well, uh, would you like to sit down at the table? Won't take me a moment to set up everything." Nervously, she poured the boiling water into her ancient, stained teapot, then covered it with a tea cozy her mother knitted forty years ago. A small plate was produced with cookies purchased from Crandall's Corner Market. "Milk or sugar?"

"Just milk, please."

When they were settled at the table, Helen studied her cup of tea while Miss Treadwell eyed her inquisitively. If the silence was to be broken, she would be the one to break it. "How long have you lived here, Helen?"

"I was born here," Helen said in a rush. "So, it'll be seventy-five years next month." Having delivered those two sentences, her eyes dropped to the table again.

"Helen." When Helen's eyes rose, Miss Treadwell said, barely above a whisper, "I think there's something you want to tell me. I'm a very good listener."

"I'm just being silly," she said for the third time. "I had a dream the second night Robbie was gone."

"What did you dream?"

"I dreamt that someone was creaking up the back stairs. But it wasn't Robbie's footsteps. Those footsteps were much lighter than his. Very light. Then I heard footsteps moving around in the apartment. In my dream, I lost track of time, so I'm not sure how long the footsteps lasted. A few moments. Maybe longer." Helen stopped there and lifted her teacup with a trembling hand.

Miss Treadwell had ceased to drink hers. Silence fell throughout the kitchen as the hand on the wall clock continued its predictable journey. Wetting her lips, she said, "Do you have any idea what time you experienced this dream?"

"About four in the morning, I think," Helen whispered, maintaining her focus on the table. Finally, she looked up. "People will laugh at me if they find out about my dream. You won't tell Myrtle, will you? I wouldn't want the girls at yoga to know about my dream."

"You can trust me, Helen. I won't reveal our conversation to any of your yoga friends," Miss Treadwell said. There were questions, but how far could she push this woman who appeared fragile and frightened? "You have a key to your house. I'm assuming Robbie has one, too."

"Yes, just the two keys."

"There's no hidden key outside in case you lock yourself out of the house?"

"No. I only leave the house once a week to go to yoga. I wouldn't do that except, well, people talk if you never leave the house. You know what I mean?" Helen said.

"Oh, yes, a small town like Bedford, people will talk."

"Robbie helped me."

"How did he help you?"

"I don't like going out," Helen said. "I mean I don't like leaving the house. It's a little scary out there."

"Yes, it can be very scary out there," Miss Treadwell said, then repeated the same question. "How did he help you?"

"Um, he moved in here and got a job at the corner market where I shop. Sometimes Mr. Crandall would deliver my things if I—if I didn't feel like going out. When Robbie moved in he asked if I'd like him to pick up a few things and bring them home for me. Then, well, it got to the place where he picked up everything for me. I never had to leave the house except for yoga." Helen hesitated, then looked up. "I paid for the groceries. Signed a check. All he had to do was fill in the amount. Some might say he cheated me, but he never did. Not once. He unpacked everything, laid it on the counter along with the bill. Insisted that I check off everything so no one could ever say he cheated me. That's the kind of young man he was."

Miss Treadwell leaned back in her chair, studying the reclusive woman who was grieving over the loss of someone who had become dear to her, and fearful of the event that had awakened her at four in the morning. "You miss Robbie."

Helen nodded as two tears slid down her face. "I miss him." She patted one of her pockets but failed to find a tissue.

Miss Treadwell opened her purse and placed a linen handkerchief beside Helen's teacup. But at that moment, a tissue was found in the opposite pocket. While Helen dabbed at her eyes, she picked up the linen handkerchief, admiring the needlework. "The edge has been beautifully crocheted by someone. I've never seen anything like it," she said. "Did you crochet the trim?"

"No but thank you. I treasure them because my mother used to crochet quite a lot. She crocheted at least a dozen linen handkerchiefs for me." Miss Treadwell returned her linen handkerchief to its proper place in her purse, then waited a moment before bringing up a subject that would cause further anxiety, yet it must be done. "Helen?" When the other woman looked up, she continued, "I'm just wondering if you'd consider having the locks on your doors changed. I know a perfectly reputable locksmith who'd be more than happy to do it for you."

Helen waited. Her head bent. Her eyes traveled back and forth across the table. "He'd have to come into the house."

"Yes, but I could come with him and perhaps we could wait in another part of the house together until he's finished."

A battle waged within Helen. A stranger in her house. If Robbie came back, he wouldn't have the right key to enter the house. But then there was the dream. "All right—Cynthia."

The two women smiled at each other for the first time. "I'll call the locksmith when I get home and schedule a time. When he comes here to do the work, I'll be with you."

"All right, Cynthia," Helen said again. "Oh, I just thought of something. There's a new lady who moved in down the street. Across from Mr. Crandall's market. She baked some cookies and brought them here when she first moved in. She's like you. I think she'd be willing to stay with me while the locksmith is here."

"A new friend." Miss Treadwell smiled. "How nice."

"Yes. I've never had a friend in my neighborhood before," Helen said.

"Helen," Miss Treadwell said. "If you have that dream again, would you call me? I mean call me as soon as the dream begins. Whenever that is, day or night."

Helen looked directly into Miss Treadwell's eyes. "Yes, I'll call you if I have that dream again."

Chapter 29

Fatigue consumed Miss Treadwell as she returned to the camera shop. Her mind sifted through and internalized the information Helen imparted. She recalled the words Helen used to describe someone creaking up the back stairs. The footsteps were light, she had said. Could it be a woman? Could it be the same woman whose images she'd captured on her camera at three o'clock in the morning? The same woman who held a gun in her hand? Could that same woman have climbed the steps at Helen's house an hour later? Was it the same night, or did Helen have her nights confused? So many questions and no answers.

After picking up the enlarged photos at the camera shop, she headed home. In no mood and too exhausted to speak to anyone, she made short work of dropping off Myrtle's groceries. Standing in her kitchen moments later, she considered dinner. Teddy and Ralph would arrive somewhere between six and six-thirty, as they did every Wednesday evening. Could she postpone it until tomorrow? She was retired. Her schedule was flexible; theirs was not.

Tonight would be a simple meal. She stood in front of the open refrigerator, considering what she could place in the crockpot. There on the second shelf was the stone with splotches of blood she'd collected when the woman fell only the night before. Had it only been a matter of hours? Seemed like weeks. She'd show it to the boys after dinner.

Selecting a few items from the refrigerator, she filled the crockpot and set it on high heat. By the time the boys arrived, dinner would be ready.

Making the promised phone call to the locksmith, she then called Helen to confirm the date. "Now, you're sure your neighbor is willing to stay with you while the locksmith changes your locks, Helen?"

"Oh, yes. I called Vera as soon as you left. She's been very nice. So interested in what's happened to Robbie. She lets me talk about him as much as I like."

"Vera. What a nice name. You don't hear that name very often anymore."

"No, I told her the same thing," Helen said. "Well, thank you so much for your help, Cynthia."

Collapsing onto her favorite chair in the living room, she drew the photos out of the envelope. Sighing, she realized he'd enlarged at least half a dozen more photos than she'd requested. Oh well, didn't matter.

She leafed idly through them until she came to the last three. Tossing the others aside, she walked to the window where the light streamed through. Unconvinced, she retrieved a magnifying glass she kept in a small table drawer beside her chair and returned to the window. She studied all three closely through the magnifying glass, then studied them again. She leaned against the window frame and closed her eyes.

Her mind drifted back to that scene. He said something as she raced to her car. Frightened, she filtered out his words. Pressing her hand to her temple, she willed her mind to interpret the words. He said, "Wait, don't leave!" What else had he said? Her eyes opened and she dropped her hand. After that, he'd said, "Wait, Miss," and her mind refused to go any farther. But she knew what the next word was. It was Treadwell. "Wait, Miss Treadwell." Guilt consumed her. Yet it was nearly dark. How could anyone recognize her. Was it a question of young eyes being much sharper as opposed to older eyes losing that capacity? Or was it the fear factor?

Miss Treadwell checked her watch, but her hand was shaking so violently she couldn't read it. She pressed her wrist against her body and noted the hour. There was still time. She'd use her landline phone, but what was the number? Leafing through her telephone directory, she punched in the numbers.

Suddenly, she wasn't at all sure her legs could support her. She fell rather than sat on her chair and listened to the ringing sound in her ear. When she heard the familiar voice, she said, "Mr. Crandall? I think I know where Robbie was as recently as last night." The shock of the information rendered the store owner silent, so Miss Treadwell continued. "At least I think I do. I just got home a few moments ago, but I'm coming back to your market as soon as I hang up. There's something you must see."

Chapter 30

Miss Treadwell added the magnifying glass to her purse before she left. She'd never done that before and wasn't sure why she did it now. A moment of foretelling perhaps? Because surely Mr. Crandall had a magnifying glass at his store. Another first was leaving her camera behind.

Adrenaline can be very useful. Adrenaline is what enabled Miss Treadwell to drive back to town and park at the same spot she had earlier that afternoon. She closed her eyes for a moment, inhaled large volumes of air, then walked to the door, grasping the envelope with the three enlarged photos inside.

Mr. Crandall met her at the door, his face drawn in confusion and worry. "What are you saying about Robbie? You saw him last night? Why didn't you mention that when you were here?" he said, attempting to keep his voice at a level of curiosity rather than accusatory.

The store was empty. Miss Treadwell led the way to the counter, drew the photos out of the envelope, and laid them side by side along with the magnifying glass. "I picked these up at the camera shop after I left Helen's house. He edited and enlarged the photos so I could see the images. I only looked at them when I got home. I called you immediately after I recognized Robbie. I should say I think it's Robbie." Having said that, she remained silent. His questions would be answered when he looked at the photos.

Mr. Crandall picked up the photos one at a time, then viewed the photos a second time through the magnifying glass. "It's Robbie, all right," he said softly. "I called Jody at the police station after you left for Helen's house. She said she'd file a missing person report. But at least now we have some idea where he was last night. I'll give her a quick call and tell her what you found."

He dialed the number and tapped his fingertips on the counter while it rang. "This is Crandall from the corner market. Is Jody nearby? I need to talk to her. She's out of the building? Know when she'll get back? Okay, well, look, when she gets back, give her a message for me. Tell her Miss Treadwell—she's Ralph Davies' mother—was out to that ruins east of town last night. Took some photos and three of them look like Robbie. I'm going out there right now to have a look around. If I find him, I'll give you a call back." He waited a moment, then said, "You got that? Okay, thanks. Be sure and give her the message, because I filed a missing person with her after he was missing for three days."

Mr. Crandall's face remained pale, but unlike earlier in the afternoon, there was a look of determination and hope about him. He untied his long, white apron, slipped it over his head, and tossed it behind the counter. "Okay, let's go."

"I beg your pardon?" Miss Treadwell said, realizing the "I" he mentioned to the police officer who answered the phone had suddenly become "we".

"You need to come with me! I don't know where you saw him. Come to think of it, I've never been there. He might be hurt and he doesn't have a car."

"He wasn't hurt last night."

"Even if he's not hurt, he can't walk twenty miles back to town. I walk to work, so you'll have to drive."

Miss Treadwell glanced at the clock behind the counter. "It's four hours until closing."

"I know it's four hours till closing. I've never closed early in the thirty-four years since I opened this store. Today, I'm closing early."

It mattered not that she'd been there early that morning as well as the previous evening, nor that she was exhausted. Drawing heavily on unknown resources, she walked out the door and tossed the photos on the floor in the back of the car. In record time, they were heading out of town. Exceeding the speed limit had never concerned Miss Treadwell before and it didn't worry her now. She cut three minutes off the time it normally took to get there.

For the third time in less than twenty-four hours, she parked in exactly the same spot beside the three deteriorating buildings. The first time, she was alone. This morning, Myrtle had accompanied her. She shoved her purse under the seat and left the keys in the ignition. They'd only be a few minutes and there was no one within miles of where they were.

Mr. Crandall hastened behind her as she retraced her steps to the place where she saw the man at the ruins sitting. "Over there," she said. "Sitting on the third step."

Now Mr. Crandall took the lead while Miss Treadwell endeavored to keep up.

They stood at opposite ends of the steps and examined every inch, moving slowly up the stairs until Mr. Crandall held out his arm. "Look," he said slowly.

Miss Treadwell drew closer and peered at the object. A small piece of paper was wedged in between the third and fourth steps. Puzzled, they continued to study it. The paper was wedged in such a manner as to be visible only if one looked closely enough. Yet, it was impossible to have happened by chance. Someone deliberately placed it there.

"Should we look at it?" Mr. Crandall said. "Police will want finger-prints if it comes to that."

"I have a pair of Ralph's evidence gloves with me," Miss Treadwell said without the slightest embarrassment. She used them to protect her camera when her hands became dirty during photoshoots. Once the evidence gloves were donned, she carefully drew out the slip of paper and held it in the palm of her hand.

"That's odd. Looks like a piece torn off of a check," Mr. Crandall said.

"A piece torn off of a check." It was identical in color and design to the one she'd photographed hours earlier at the edge of the cliff. Identical but how could they be so far removed from each other? She glanced up to the top of the cliff. Then, for the second time within the hour, Miss Treadwell's legs began to fail her. Using the rail for support, she lowered her body to the third step.

"You all right?" Mr. Crandall said solicitously.

"Something dreadful is happening here and I have no idea what it is."

Chapter 31

Mr. Crandall was about to question her when another item caught his eye. It was a coin tucked in the corner of the step. Within its protective shadow, the color of the coin blended in with its surroundings. "Would you give me your glove," he said. Slipping on the glove, he studied one side of the coin, flipped it over, and inspected the reverse side. Having done that, he eased his body down on the step opposite Miss Treadwell.

His face had paled significantly from when he looked at the photos at the corner market thirty minutes ago. "What is it?" she whispered. His eyes were vacant, so she touched his shoulder. "Mr. Crandall, what is it?"

His eyes slowly met hers. "Do you remember I said I was a coin collector? When Robbie showed an interest, I helped him get started collecting them." When Miss Treadwell nodded, he continued, "I gave him this nickel the last night he worked at the store."

"Are you sure?"

"Positive. It's fairly rare. I'm embarrassed to say I wanted to keep this coin and very nearly didn't give it to him."

"Do you remember how many coins you gave him?"

"Twelve. I think I mentioned that at the store," Mr. Crandall said softly.

"Yes, you did. I just wanted to be sure," she said. "When I searched through Robbie's apartment, I saw the coin box and took the liberty of opening it. There were only eleven coins. So, the day you gave Robbie this coin, he must not have returned to his apartment."

"He folded the coin in a tissue then put it in his pocket before he left the store," Mr. Crandall said. "Do you think he left it here on purpose, hoping someone would find it and eventually I'd be able to identify it as the one I gave him?"

How to respond? Mr. Crandall clung to the hope inspired by finding the coin. "I do believe you're right. But there's more."

"What do you mean?"

"I looked through Robbie's calendar. The night he disappeared he was scheduled to meet someone at Teddy's Café at six o'clock. You know my eldest son owns the café."

"Yes, I know your son owns the café. I've been there a number of times. Robbie must have gone directly from the store to the café," he said. "Did you ask Teddy about it?"

"Yes. He said Robbie came to the café alone. He was waiting for someone, but the woman never arrived so he left."

Mr. Crandall's brows drew together. "A woman? He never mentioned anything about a girlfriend or anything like that. He was a bit of a loner like Helen. I think that's one reason they got along so well. They understood each other."

They sat in silence, immersed in their own thoughts. Miss Treadwell was the first to speak. "If Robbie is still here, where could he possibly be?"

Mr. Crandall stood while his eyes surveyed the ruins. "He may be hurt, waiting for help."

"But he had to hear us. Don't you think he would have called out when we first arrived?"

"Maybe he can't call out. Looking for him is worth a try."

There were three buildings and they canvassed every one thoroughly as the store owner repeatedly called Robbie's name. Standing outside the third building, their eyes traveled beyond the perimeter of the ruins to the path behind them, then rose to the top of the cliff.

"If he's still here, he could be anywhere," Miss Treadwell said. She felt the lack of sleep and emotional rollercoaster she'd endured for the past twenty-four hours. Slowly, she turned, retracing her steps to the car.

Mr. Crandall refused to move. "We can't give up now."

Miss Treadwell glanced at her watch. Mr. Crandall was in deep distress and he needed her support. "This is an enormous area. We need help."

Mr. Crandall bit down on a mouth determined to find the young man he'd grown so fond of. "Let's give it a little more time. If we haven't found him, we'll call for help," he said, then gazed behind the buildings. "Let's start with the path at the bottom of the cliff. If we don't find him there, we'll drive to the top and continue our search."

Miss Treadwell felt her throat tighten as she remembered the previous evening.

Her peripheral vision sensed motion and she turned her head. He moved rapidly through the darkened shadows. That's how she knew someone was walking along the path below a wall that rose sharply behind the ruins. Had he remained stationary, he would have blended in with the surroundings. It was an unsettling feeling, thinking she was safely alone only to see a figure moving swiftly along the path. Had he seen her? She thought not. Hoped not.

Suddenly, she felt vulnerable. There was a certain level of charm in being alone with the mystique of the ruins as darkness settled in, which would be lost had she brought someone with her. Yet that mystique quickly evolved from charm to concern, even worry. She was alone in a deserted place with someone quietly and quickly making his way along a path she hadn't known existed.

When she didn't respond, Mr. Crandall said, "Miss Treadwell?"

But what if the man she saw walking along the path was Robbie and he was taking a perfectly innocent walk that she misinterpreted? Yet he didn't have a car. So who was the person chasing her last night? "All right, Mr. Crandall," she said, trying but failing to keep her voice steady. "We'll try the path first. If Robbie isn't there, we'll drive up to the cliff area."

As they left the ruins to search along the path behind the three buildings, a car drove slowly by and parked on the far side of the ruins, out of view of any passersby. But so focused were they on finding the young man, that neither Miss Treadwell nor Mr. Crandall heard it.

Chapter 32

Humans have been imbued with the gift of instinct for a reason. Instinct is what warns them that something is amiss or they're in danger. In his eagerness to find Robbie, Mr. Crandall ignored that gift. Miss Treadwell did not. She sensed invisible eyes were upon them. She continually searched the area. What she failed to do was look up to the top of the cliff.

Mr. Crandall walked mindlessly ahead along the path while Miss Treadwell trailed a few yards behind. She checked her watch again, thought of her dinner, and her boys, then looked over her shoulder, searching and listening. Not wanting the burden of carrying anything, she'd left her purse in the car tucked underneath the driver's seat. Her phone was in that purse, which she now regretted not bringing with her. A quick call would allay any fears they may have of finding the house empty when they arrived. Well, this shouldn't take long. Once they returned to the car, she'd make the calls.

She began to feel sluggish, light-headed from the low blood sugar of not having eaten for four hours. Normally she ate four or five small meals each day rather than three larger ones. With only three hours sleep the night before, she lagged even farther behind. But it was more than lack of sleep. It was the fear generated by finding someone in a deserted place the evening before and being chased by a car. It was the deeply unsettling experience of being awakened in the middle of the night by prowlers in her neighbor's driveway. And it was saving Myrtle from certain death, knowing it was not an accident. All of it in less than twenty-four hours. Perhaps she should call ahead and tell Mr. Crandall she'd sit on the side of the path and rest a bit. He could join her when he finished searching for Robbie along the path.

Suddenly, Mr. Crandall stopped walking. His body stood tense and she heard a muffled cry. Once again, adrenaline took hold and she moved rapidly forward till she reached his side, then drew her hand to her mouth. Fifteen feet ahead lay the body of a man. His back was to them. In his heightened state of anxiety, Mr. Crandall assumed it was Robbie.

"No, no, no," Mr. Crandall whispered, his hands pressed against the sides of his face.

Miss Treadwell placed a comforting hand on his shoulder. "I'll…" she began. "I'll just have a quick look. You wait here."

But Mr. Crandall was raised old school. He could not allow someone else to assume a responsibility that should be his. "No, I'll go." He stepped forward, balancing his weight from tree trunk to tree trunk until he stood over the body. Turning to face Miss Treadwell, he said in a halting voice, "It's not Robbie. I—I don't know who this is."

Using the same tactics as Mr. Crandall, Miss Treadwell used the trees to brace herself as she made her way to his side. He was somewhere in his mid-forties. At a guess, he was six feet tall and had enjoyed his food perhaps to a greater degree than he should have. She shook her head. She didn't recognize him either. "I need to call Ralph," she said in a shallow voice.

"Your phone's in the car," Mr. Crandall said, his voice equally hollow. They'd covered twenty feet when he sensed Miss Treadwell begin to fail.

"Yes, it's in the…." This time, when her legs gave out, there was no chair or step to support her, and she crumpled to the ground with Mr. Crandall breaking her fall the last two feet.

He dropped to his knees and touched her shoulder, then looked up. Someone was moving rapidly down the path toward them. He didn't recognize him, but perhaps he would offer help. Or was he the reason for the body that lay behind them?

"Has she fainted?" the man said solicitously. "She must be ill. Let me help you." He felt the pulse in Miss Treadwell's neck and drew back her eyelid. "Seems steady enough. What happened?"

Mr. Crandall was in as much shock as Miss Treadwell and felt light-headed. He hadn't eaten since lunchtime either, but he'd had a full night's sleep. However, finding a dead body is traumatic, and the shock he suffered was visible on his pale face and somewhat vacant expression. "There's a—a body back there," he said, casting a glance over his shoulder.

"A body? A man's dead? Did you recognize him?"

In his shock, it didn't occur to Mr. Crandall that the stranger knew the gender of the body. "No, I don't know who he is."

"I'll just take a look," the stranger said. He stood over the body a few seconds before returning. "No idea who he is either," he said, shaking his head.

"We were about to call the police when you arrived, but her phone is in her car," Mr. Crandall said, failing to notice the stranger was the only one of the three who registered no shock.

"Can't make any calls right here. We're in a dead zone," he said with such assurance that Mr. Crandall didn't question him. "We'll call when we're far enough away from here to get a signal." He continued to observe Miss Treadwell. "My younger sister is a nurse. We're vacationing nearby. Let's take your friend there until she feels better." The man didn't wait for Mr. Crandall's approval. He slid one hand under her back and the other one under her knees and lifted her effortlessly. He walked hurriedly down the path, then turned right toward the parking lot.

When they reached Miss Treadwell's car, the man peered inside, noting the key was in the ignition. There was a manilla envelope tossed carelessly on the back floor. "Open the door," he said. "You can hold onto her while I drive you to the house where my sister and I are staying."

Mr. Crandall's mind was numb. He blindly obeyed without questioning the man's name or who he was or where he was from. Later, he'd wonder where this man's car was. How did he arrive at the ruins?

He climbed into the backseat and supported Miss Treadwell while the man started the car without revving it. He backed up quietly, almost soundlessly. Once on Cliff Road, he pressed down on the accelerator.

Mr. Crandall lifted his chin and watched the speedometer climb to seventy miles per hour. A careful driver, his mouth was dry, hoping no one would spring out in front of them from some unknown side road.

Miss Treadwell's eyes fluttered and her lips moved. Mr. Crandall positioned his ear near her mouth. "What happened?" she said weakly.

"You fainted after we found the body on the path," he said in her ear.

"A body? Oh, yes," she said faintly. "It wasn't Robbie."

"No," Mr. Crandall said in a relieved voice. "It wasn't Robbie. We don't know who it is."

"Is this my car?" When Mr. Crandall nodded, she said," "Who's driving it?"

Mr. Crandall studied the back of the man who sped needlessly down the narrow road. He shook his head and whispered in her ear, "I don't know."

"Where are we going?"

"I don't know that either."

Chapter 33

Within five minutes, he turned onto a road with a sign that read, "No Exit". He passed a deserted house with a shed at the end of the driveway.

From the time they left the ruins until they pulled off the main road, Miss Treadwell opened her eyes several times and lifted her head to look outside, but she appeared disoriented and confused even though the words she uttered made sense. Her brow furrowed as they passed the abandoned house with a driveway leading back to a shed.

"I think I was here last night."

Mr. Crandall saw her lips move and bent his ear to her mouth.

"I think I was here last night," she repeated.

What did she mean by that? He was about to ask her when her eyes closed and her head slid to the side.

The man rounded a bend and pulled into a house surrounded by fields. It stood alone and isolated. The nearest neighbor was the abandoned house.

Mr. Crandall's eyes swept the area. Vacationing? He was deeply puzzled. It wasn't the kind of place people chose to vacation.

The man pocketed Miss Treadwell's car keys as he walked up to the front door and unlocked it. He opened it a few inches and peered around the corner before returning to the car. He gathered Miss Treadwell in his arms and carried her into the house with Mr. Crandall lagging behind, still unable to think clearly.

Was he overreacting to the stranger's generous offer to help? Miss Treadwell was a good sounding board and he badly needed to discuss this situation with her. But in her current condition, she could offer no support. This man appeared to be making every effort to help them, yet he intuitively felt something wasn't right. Where was his sister's car, or did they only have one car?

"My sister seems to have disappeared for a while. Probably drove into town for groceries or something. There's a downstairs bedroom. I'll put her in there."

Mr. Crandall surveyed the first room. It was a fairly large and squarish. There were four windows. Two were on either side of the door and two windows faced the east. There was another room to the right of the main one and he spied a kitchen at the end of the hallway. All the windows had venetian blinds that were closed. It was the same when he joined the man in the bedroom. Two windows faced the east and they also had venetian blinds which were closed. It had obviously been a dining room at one time because a chandelier hung from the ceiling in the middle of the room. But it had been raised until it was nearly flush with the ceiling.

Mr. Crandall had done some remodeling of his corner market a number of times, so he recognized the signs of plaster that had not dried completely. This room had been recently converted from a dining room to a bedroom. But why?

"I'll fetch some soup. Do both of you a world of good. My sister shouldn't be gone long."

"I need to get her purse from the car," Mr. Crandall said.

"Right, I'll get it now then heat up your soup." The stranger walked through the front door and closed it. He knew where the purse was because his foot touched it when he adjusted the seat back to give him more leg room. He opened the car door, but something caught his eye in the backseat. It was the manilla envelope he'd seen earlier. Peering over his shoulder at the narrow windows on either side of the door, he picked it up and viewed the contents. Three photos. He slid the manilla envelope underneath his shirt, picked up the purse and returned to the house, locking the door, and pocketing the key before heading to the kitchen. "Soup won't take a minute," he said before disappearing out of view.

Mr. Crandall was about to ask for the purse, but the man was well into the hallway before he uttered the first word. Why make the effort to get the purse yet not give it to its owner?

Even though her eyes remained closed, Miss Treadwell was conscious because her head moved back and forth on the pillow. Mr. Crandall shifted his attention from the purse to the woman on the bed. He sat beside her and touched her arm. When she opened her eyes, he softly repeated what he'd said earlier. "You fainted while we were on the pathway. A stranger came along and brought us to the house he and his sister are renting. He's gone into the kitchen to get some soup for us."

Miss Treadwell tried and failed to sit up. Mr. Crandall rearranged the pillows and helped her into a sitting position. She closed her eyes again and they remained closed until the stranger came into the room carrying a tray with two bowls of soup and several slices of bread.

"This should help both of you." He sat in a chair, watching them eat for a moment, then said casually, "I called the police and reported the body. Gave them specifics about where it is. They have my phone number. I'll need to leave shortly to join them at the ruins." Having said that, he rose and left the room.

Mr. Crandall said nothing as he finished his soup and bread. He heard the stranger moving things in the kitchen. What he hadn't heard was his voice talking to the police.

A few moments later, the man returned and stood in the doorway to the bedroom. He'd changed clothes. Along the path, he wore a pair of slacks and a polo shirt. Why did he change into a suit, white shirt, and dress shoes? Were those cufflinks? Yes, and a kerchief in his breast pocket as well. It was so illogical Miss Treadwell's mind appeared to rebound and she stared at the man, who smiled at them. He appeared benign, helpful, yet there was something about him she couldn't define. That would come later.

"I need to leave now. You know how it is. I promised the police I'd meet them. My sister shouldn't be long," he reminded them. Before they could respond, he crossed the front room, unlocked the door, and left. They heard him insert the key from the other side of the door and lock it again.

The door was nearly closed when Mr. Crandall called out, "What about a key?" But the door closed, was locked, and they heard him start the car.

Chapter 34

"He didn't tell us if there's another key in the house," Mr. Crandall said, putting his tray aside and trotting to the door. He attempted to turn the doorknob even though the man was pulling out of the driveway. He knew it was a deadbolt lock and required a key to open it. There wasn't a key hanging on a nearby hook. He peered through the small window in the door for several moments, then slowly returned to the bedroom and sat in his chair. "He headed in the wrong direction. The sign on the main road said No Exit. I waited to see if he'd turn around and come back, but he didn't. Why did he turn that way if he can't get out?"

Miss Treadwell remembered a blurry vision of the No Exit sign. "Ralph will surely be at the ruins shortly. He'll see that man is driving my car. But how will he get to the ruins if he turned the wrong way?" Then another thought occurred to her. "My purse. Where is it? I need to call Ralph and tell him what's happened."

"That stranger brought it in. Must be in the kitchen." He returned shortly and handed it to her.

Miss Treadwell looked inside and dumped its contents onto the bed beside where she sat. The impossible can be difficult to accept. She looked in her purse again, pressing the sides together with her hands in case the phone was lodged in a dark corner. "It's gone," she said, then stated the obvious. "He took it." As they stared at each other, the same question was reflected in their eyes. Why would he take her phone?

"He doesn't want us to contact anyone," Mr. Crandall said. "Maybe there's a phone somewhere in the house."

"I very much doubt it. If he took my phone because he doesn't want us to contact anyone, he'd surely not leave a house phone available for our use."

Even so, they split up and covered the downstairs, looking for a landline phone. When they met in the front room again it was obvious they both had failed to find one.

"There was a phone on the kitchen wall, but it's been removed," Miss Treadwell said. "I tried the kitchen door but it's locked, too."

"I wonder how recently the phone was removed?"

"I thought the same thing."

They sat on opposite ends of the sofa, immersed in their own thoughts.

"Do you think it odd that he would change into dress clothes to meet the police at the ruins?"

Mr. Crandall considered the question. "Yes, it is strange. I wonder why he did that."

"Why did he lock both doors and why did he take my phone? Obviously we're his prisoners, but why?"

"Why imprison people you only met an hour ago?" Mr.

Crandall said.

"And we can't call for help without a phone," Miss Treadwell said.

"We can climb through a window. There were several steps up to the house, so it would be a quite a drop, except for the windows on either side of the door."

They crossed the front room and opened the venetian blinds to the left of the door. Behind them was a wide, tall window. Neither of them spoke as they stared at the window. It seemed an eternity before Mr. Crandall said, "Why did he do this?"

There were vertical, metal bars placed at six-inch intervals. Mr. Crandall checked the other three windows in that room while Miss Treadwell returned to the bedroom. All the windows in both rooms had bars on them. They split up, each going to another room downstairs. Miss Treadwell made her way down the hall to the kitchen again while Mr. Crandall checked the fourth room, which was virtually empty.

There was a window over the kitchen sink and a window in the door leading to the backyard. Both had bars on them. In desperation, she searched every drawer and cupboard for a key to the backdoor, then walked into the pantry and checked the shelves. As a last resort, she inspected the refrigerator and freezer compartment. She felt her way along the countertop to the nearest chair and sat down. The question arose again. Why?

There was an abundance of food in the refrigerator and freezer. There was enough canned goods and boxes of prepared food to last the stranger and his sister a month. It was as though a winter storm was approaching and they had stocked up in the event they were trapped.

Having finished with the kitchen, she made her way back to the front room where neither said a word. Their faces spoke volumes.

The soup gave them a few moments' reprieve from their initial shock and exhaustion. But the revelation that the stranger had taken her phone, making outside communication impossible, then left without leaving a key depleted their remaining reserves. The fact that he intended to make them prisoners was daunting and inexplicable. They had suffered a setback and needed to rest before tackling the second floor.

Resettled on the sofa, Miss Treadwell rested her elbow on the arm and supported her chin while she searched her memory banks. "I've seen him before," she began. "But where?"

Chapter 35

Leto turned right instead of left out of the driveway. It didn't matter whether or not the two prisoners saw him. There was nothing they could do about it. Had he covered all his bases? Was there any chance they could escape? Taking a moment to think through the steps he'd taken, he knew he was safe.

He had to avoid the main road because he had no idea who or when someone would find the body or when they'd call the police. Hopefully not until he was safely settled in his hotel room.

Driving another half mile, he turned onto a seldom-used dirt path just wide enough to accommodate the old car's tires.

The dirt path led into the woods and eventually began to climb. It leveled off for a quarter of a mile then made a sharp turn. Just before he negotiated the turn, he pulled in between two trees. It was critical that the car not be found, otherwise all would be lost. He tossed the manilla envelope containing the three photos in the back, slid the keys underneath the seat, and ran the remaining one hundred feet of the journey.

Rounding the corner, the maintenance building stood before him. Just as he'd thought, Hannah and Job eventually unlocked the main door and came out hoping to escape. He'd waited just out of sight, grabbed the girl, and forced Job to drive his car to the house where they presently resided with the two older people. Now, he pressed through the door and strode to the rented car he'd used the entire time he was in Bedford.

"What took you so long?" Hannah said.

"Just did, that's all."

"Any problems?"

"None," Leto said.

"Why did you object to those two older people finding the body?"

"The body needs to be discovered after I'm at the hotel rather than when I'm a few feet away from it. Those two were going to call the police. Couldn't take the chance."

"I don't understand why you moved the body from where it originally landed on the path?"

"I already explained why." Leto stared at her as he would a child who couldn't remember simple explanations. "I needed to hide the body while I searched for the pieces of the checks. What if I couldn't find all of them? So the body had to be moved. After I hid him, I cleaned up and smoothed out the entire area where he landed. I couldn't allow them to find evidence that he was there for a few hours."

"But there's no evidence he fell over the cliff and landed at the place those people found him."

"Do you think I wouldn't plan for that? I drove up to the cliff parking lot and rolled a limb over the edge directly in front of Grayson's parked car. I needed to see where it would land once it got to the path. And that's where I put him. Don't you see? His car is parked there and his body is found right below on the path. The police will think suicide," he said. "Okay? Any more questions?"

Hannah resented the tone of his voice. "You can't keep those people prisoners forever. So what do you plan to do with them?"

Leto lifted an eyebrow, then turned his back on her and opened two doors wide enough to allow mowing equipment to drive through. He got into his car and said, "Change your clothes and be ready in case I need to call you."

He headed into the woods past where Miss Treadwell's car was hidden. He picked up speed, racing past the house where he'd just deposited the two prisoners and made his way to Cliff Road. At this point, he pressed down on the accelerator, hoping to get to the hotel in Bedford before someone found the body and called the police. When the police arrived at the ruins, it was critical for him to be out of the area. He'd enter the hotel the back way and leave through the front door when the police called, making sure to speak to the desk clerk and remark on the time. No one would know when he arrived at the hotel, but they could testify when he left.

Chapter 36

Two brothers found him as they rounded a curve along the path directly below the edge of the cliff. At a distance, they thought he might have tripped and fallen. There were hidden roots under layers of leaves and scanty grass where more than one person had suffered injury. But as the twelve- and ten-year-old boys drew nearer, the man didn't move.

Their curiosity was morbidly piqued yet terrified of what they suspected. They settled on a game of rock paper scissors. The loser would step forward and awaken the man. Yet both boys feared no amount of jostling his shoulder would bring this man out of his eternal sleep. His reclining posture was all wrong for resting.

The loser of the game stepped forward bravely if slowly. He stooped a distance from where the man lay, reached out at arm's length, and placed his hand on the man's shoulder. He gave it a gentle shake, but there was no reaction.

Hoping for the best, he said in a thin, tentative voice, "You okay,

Mister?" When there was no response, he placed both hands on his shoulder and shook harder. That's when the man rolled over. The boy covered his nose and backed up. His focus fixed on the man who stared at the sky with unseeing eyes.

While a small group gathered around the body, one person stood at the top of the cliff, witnessing the first stage of their plan unfold.

Karl Farrell walked rapidly down the hallway to Lieutenant Davies' office, tapped on the door, and walked in. Ralph never responded to knocks on his door. Everyone knew to tap on his door before entering. "Ralph."

It was the tone of Karl's voice that made Ralph look up sharply. "What is it, Karl?"

"A couple of kids, brothers, found a body at the bottom of the cliff behind the ruins east of town. One of the boys just called. The older one. Name's Peter Miller."

"How old are the brothers?"

"Twelve and ten."

"Were any adults with the kids?"

"It was a family outing, so there were five people, but the parents were a distance from the scene. The younger boy left to get them. Peter stayed with the body. Apparently, one of the parents gave the boys a phone because they were setting up a picnic and didn't want the kids to stray too far."

"What did the boy say?"

"He said there were no signs of bullet holes, stab wounds, or anything like that. One more thing. The kid said there was no identification on the body."

Ralph grimaced as he rose from his chair. "So, he moved the body."

"Yep, he moved the body."

"I wonder if the body is Grayson Matthews."

"Hope not," Karl said, vocalizing what they both thought. A well-known figure like that would create an uproar in the media. Journalists would swarm Bedford County. It would take time away from the investigation.

"Okay. Pull a team together. I'll call for a crime scene tech." Ralph punched in a number that led directly to Sam's personal phone. "Sam?"

Sam took a few minutes to study the three photos of the man at the ruins before she left to go home. The young man looked familiar, but she couldn't put her finger on where she may have seen him. When her phone buzzed, she noticed it was Ralph. He rarely called her this time of day unless it was police business. "Hi, Ralph."

"Sam, a couple of kids found a body behind the ruins east of town. We're pulling a team together right now."

"If you need a crime tech, I'm available. I can be there in a few minutes."

"Thanks. We'll leave shortly after I brief the Chief. Hopefully that won't take long." Ralph ended the call and stepped into the hall, where he saw Jody among the group of officers involved in Karl's briefing. He gave Karl a moment to finish the briefing, then caught her eye and she walked up to him. "You heard about the body behind the ruins?"

"I just got back. I saw Karl briefing everyone so I joined the group."

"Did Karl mention the two people who found the body are kids?"

"Yes. Karl said they're brothers. Twelve and ten. The older brother is

Peter Miller. I might know Peter. The last three summers I've coached boys' soccer. A boy named Peter Miller was on the team. It's not an uncommon name so it could be someone else."

"Good. I was going to ask you to interview the boys. Since you might know one of them, it's an even stronger reason for you to be the person conducting the interviews."

"I understand. He's very young. He'll feel more comfortable with someone he knows."

"Right. They're probably in shock, so we'll see how it goes," Ralph said. "I realize you just got back, but I need you to leave immediately. We always separate people before they put their heads together and come up with the same story. Since this is a family, it's probably too late for that, but, as I said, they may still be in shock."

"Okay, I'm on my way."

"Oh, Jody, take someone with you."

Jody nodded then stopped midstride. "Ralph, I spoke to the hotel manager about the missing hotel clerk. The whole story is a little odd. I got the desk clerk's address as well as where I could find the landlord. The landlord has no idea where she is. Like the manager reported, she disappeared the same day Grayson Matthews did. I didn't ask to see her apartment. Thought I'd better run that past you first."

"Right, we'll consider that later," Ralph said. "So it's a young woman who disappeared. Karl didn't get far enough into the interview with the hotel manager to get many details."

"Her name is Hannah. Hannah Bennett. She claims to be twenty. Although, I'm not sure that's her real name or age."

"What makes you think that?"

"Hotel manager said she seemed like a nice kid. Hannah claimed her purse with all her identification in it was stolen. She'd applied for replacements but they hadn't come yet. She worked for him a few weeks and did such a good job, he forgot about it."

"Paid her under the table to avoid paying taxes, I suspect."

"I thought the same thing. He seemed very nervous about it when I asked him," Jody said. "When I spoke to the landlord, he said Hannah had lived there about a month. Good tenant. Paid cash for her rent. No problems. The landlord called the hotel manager. Neither one can give any reason for her disappearance."

"No trace of her. Disappeared for no obvious reason and at the same time as Grayson Matthews. There has to be a connection. If we only knew what it was."

Chapter 37

"Do you want me to follow up on the Hannah Bennett situation?" Jody said.

"Yes, a little later. I need you to keep those five people from doing any more damage than they've already done," Ralph said, then tapped on Chief Henderson's door and waited. Here, permission to enter was required.

"Come in," Chief Henderson barked.

"Sir," Ralph said, not bothering to sit down. "Karl got a call from Peter Miller, a twelve-year-old boy. He and his ten-year-old brother found a body at the bottom of the cliff at the ruins. No information other than the kid didn't see any obvious bullet holes or stab wounds. Searched the body for identification and didn't find that either," he said, keeping his voice as neutral as possible.

Chief Henderson yanked out an unlit cigar from his mouth and threw it forcefully into the trash can. "He did what?! Never mind. Hard to tell how much damage they've done. Don't they watch enough TV to know you're not supposed to contaminate the crime scene?" Chief Henderson snarled. "Got a crime tech yet?"

"Yes, sir. Samantha McKean is on her way."

Ralph turned to leave, but the Chief became pensive. "Something else, sir?"

"That VIP who's missing. Grayson Matthews. I wonder if the body could be his."

"Hope not," Ralph said, echoing Karl's sentiments.

"I hope not, too," the Chief said. "Problem I have is the best fishing streams are in Cameron County. So what's he doing up here? I can't buy the story that he came up here just to fish."

"You think he used fishing as a cover to come up here?"

"I do. We just don't know why he needed a cover."

Ralph headed for the back door where his car was parked when he heard his name called. The officer covering the front desk hurried toward him.

"I thought I heard Jody's voice."

"Yes, she was here for a few minutes but left for the ruins," Ralph said.

"I was on the phone so had to wait until I was finished," the officer said. "Mr. Crandall called. He owns the corner market."

"Yes, I know who you mean," Ralph said, hoping the officer would get to the point. "What about him?"

"He called and left a message for her." He read from his notes, "Miss Treadwell—she's Ralph Davies' mother—was out to that ruins east of town last night. Took some photos and three of them look like Robbie.

I'm going out there right now to have a look around. If I find him, I'll give you a call back. Be sure and give her the message, because I filed a missing person with her after he was missing for three days."

When did that call come in?" Ralph said, keeping the urgency out of his voice.

"About an hour ago, but Jody was gone so I had to wait till she got back."

She was last seen at Crandall's Corner Market. The message jolted Ralph, but he maintained an outward appearance of equilibrium. "An hour ago," he murmured.

"What was that, Ralph?"

Ralph looked up. "Oh, nothing. I tried to call my mother earlier and she didn't answer her phone, so she must have left it in the car. That's all," he said. "Okay, so three of the photos look like Robbie?"

"That's what Mr. Crandall claims," the officer said. "Robbie went missing three days ago. Jody lives near his store and shops there every week, so they know each other. That's why he called her to file a missing person report."

"Three days. He's been missing as long as Grayson Matthews and Hannah Bennett."

"You'll probably see Mr. Crandall once you get there."

"Another person at the ruins we'll have to deal with," Ralph said.

"Right."

"Okay, thanks. I'm headed out to the ruins as soon as Samantha McKean gets here. Give Jody a call and relay that message to her."

But as he slid behind the wheel of his car, he reviewed the message. He was a strong believer that there were few coincidences in police work. His mother was at the ruins taking photos last night. Some of the photos looked like Robbie, who works at Crandall's Corner Market. He went missing the same time as Grayson Matthews and Hannah Bennett. Now there was a body at the ruins. Hopefully it wasn't the young man who worked for Mr. Crandall. And finally, at least he knew where his mother had been an hour ago.

Chapter 38

Teddy kept his eye on the clock the entire afternoon. At four thirty, two of his staff walked through the backdoor and he decided to leave for his mother's house a little earlier than usual.

Ten minutes later, he pulled into the place he thought of as home. His mother always left the front door unlocked on Wednesday when she knew her boys would arrive. But the door was locked. Teddy rang the doorbell. When there was no answer, he fumbled for the housekey attached to his keyring then unlocked it. The heartwarming aroma of dinner wafted from the kitchen down the hallway. Smiling, he called out as he made his way to the kitchen.

The kitchen was empty. That had never happened before and he stood nonplussed as his eyes swept back and forth several times, convinced he'd missed something. Perhaps it was the chef in him, but he checked the crockpot, giving the contents a couple of stirs, testing to see how much more time it needed. He moved on to the refrigerator. His brows drew together as he studied what looked like part of a brick. He carried it to the window.

The plastic bag was clear, so he saw the blood stain on the corner of the light-colored brick. There was writing on the bag. It was Mom's writing. The time she'd written was three thirty in the morning. She'd collected it from the brick-lined edging at Myrtle's house. Whose blood was it and why had she felt compelled to collect it at three thirty in the morning?

Teddy's mind froze as he continued to stare at the blood-stained brick. He had to keep moving if he was to find his mother. Her bedroom was on the main floor. Her bedroom door was open. A quick search came up negative. She must be upstairs. He called her name, but there was no response. Perhaps she was hurt. Undefinable fear gripped him. He took the stairs two at a time.

Slowly, he descended the steps. The basement? But she wasn't there either. In any case, she would have heard him moving around on the main floor.

The garage. He went out the backdoor, noting that her car keys were missing from the hook beside the door. Her keys were missing and so was her car.

He knocked on Myrtle Martin's door. His hands were trembling, so he stuffed them inside his pockets.

"Teddy," Myrtle said, surprised to see him.

"Hi, Mrs. Martin," Teddy said, always addressing her formally. "Uh, I don't suppose you've seen my mother today? She's not home."

"Not home?" Myrtle said, checking her watch. "She should be getting dinner ready."

"Well, it's in the crockpot. But, uh, well, she's not there."

"I see," Myrtle said vaguely. "Well, she stopped here about two thirty or so, I think. Can't be sure."

"Did she come in for tea or anything?"

"No, she got groceries for me at Crandall's Corner Market. It's downtown. You probably know him."

"Yes," Teddy said hurriedly. "Mr. Crandall's been to the café a few times."

"Yes, well, Cynthia was in an all-fire hurry to tell you the truth. Hardly said a word. Just helped me put the groceries away then bustled right out the door."

"Did she mention going anywhere else?"

"No, but I saw her leave again about twenty or thirty minutes later," Myrtle said, then hastened to add, "Just happened to be in the front room and saw her leave. Which reminds me, Teddy. You and Ralph really need to talk to your mother about getting that fender repaired. I don't know how she is ever going to find a garage who can match that shade of blue." She inhaled deeply, ready for round two, when Teddy assured her he and Ralph would take care of it.

With a hurried word of thanks, he headed back to the house. He paced from the kitchen down the hallway and into the living room while he gave his mother ten more minutes, then he'd call Ralph. When ten minutes passed, he punched in his brother's number. Before Teddy could say anything, Ralph spoke.

"Teddy," Ralph said, closing his eyes. "I forgot all about dinner with Mom tonight. Tell her I'm really sorry. Something has come up and I won't be able to make it." He was about to explain about the body, knowing the information wouldn't go any further, when Teddy cut him off.

"Ralph! I'm at the house. Mom isn't here. Myrtle Martin said she was downtown. Well, you already know she and Sam had lunch together. Mom stopped at Crandall's Corner Market after lunch because she dropped off groceries at Mrs. Martin's house about two thirty. She saw Mom leave the house a little later. She put dinner in the crockpot then left and didn't come back. I don't know where she is."

Ralph sat in his car, waiting for Sam to arrive. "She didn't leave a note."

"No, she didn't leave a note," Teddy said, then wondered if he should bring up the blood-stained brick. As much as it puzzled him, the fact that their mother was missing took priority.

"Okay, take a careful look around the house and see what you can find. There may be some small detail that will give us a clue," Ralph said, wondering if there was a possibility that she joined Mr. Crandall in his search for Robbie at the ruins. He toyed with sharing his concern with his brother but decided Teddy had enough to worry about. "Look, some kids discovered a man's body on the path behind the ruins. I'll be out there but I'll have my phone on me, so give me a call," he said. "Call me whether you find anything, no matter how insignificant it is. Okay?"

"Okay, Ralph. I'll see what I can find and call you." Teddy's eyes surveyed the living room. Returning to the front door, he began his search room by room and inch by inch. He'd seen the stack of photos when he first arrived. But he was accustomed to a stack of photos. Ralph said there may be some small detail, so he sat down and examined them. They were unlike anything she'd ever taken. Photos of uprooted grass, a corner of what appeared to be a check, but what were the other photos?

A magnifying glass was what he needed. But when he searched the drawer where his mother kept it, it was missing. His mother was fastidious about returning things to their proper place lest they get lost.

There was the outline of a car which appeared to be taken from the living room window in the middle of the night. Then there were photos of someone leaving the car, running in front of Mrs. Martin's white siding, and returning.

The next photo was of someone sitting on the ground in front of the siding, holding her hand, for it looked like a woman. She must have fallen and been injured. There was a lighter object surrounding her hand. A tissue? Had she bled? Teddy's eyes lifted. Blood. The refrigerator.

He reviewed all the photos again. Had his mother told her neighbor about the photos taken in her driveway? He couldn't just sit here. With the photos in hand, he trotted between the peony bushes with the intent of knocking on Mrs. Martin's door. But curiosity stopped him in front of the white siding. His eyes traced the bricks that outlined the narrow garden planted the width of the house. There it was. The tops of all the bricks were clean except for one. It had been buried in the dirt a short time ago. Teddy bent and plucked the brick out of the dirt. One corner had been chipped away and it now resided in his mother's refrigerator.

Replacing the brick, he walked rapidly down the sidewalk and stood at the front door.

When Mrs. Martin opened the door, her brows rose slightly. "Teddy, why are you back so soon? Has something happened?"

"I need to talk to you. I need to talk right now."

Mrs. Martin widened the door and allowed him to enter. She led him into the living room and sat down. "Won't you sit down, Teddy?"

But Teddy couldn't sit down. He knelt in front of her and handed her the edited, enlarged photos. "Did Mom show these to you?"

Mrs. Martin's hands shook as she viewed each photo in turn. When she finished, she looked up. "She told me there were prowlers sneaking around my house about three o'clock in the morning last night, but I didn't see the photos. We went out to the ruins early this morning. Cynthia was there taking photos last night and something happened that upset her. I persuaded her to return to ease her mind. She told me about the prowlers as we pulled out of my driveway." Her mouth opened and closed several times, but nothing came out.

There it was again. The ruins. "Mrs. Martin," Teddy said softly. "What is it?"

"It's all my fault. If only I'd followed Cynthia's advice you wouldn't be here right now." She reached for the tissue she always kept in her pocket and pressed it to her eyes.

Teddy paled. "What happened?" he whispered. When she hesitated, he said, "Tell me."

"Teddy, I want you to sit down and I'll tell you everything. Then you need to call Ralph."

Chapter 39

Sam pulled into the parking lot, stowed crime scene equipment in the trunk of Ralph's car and slid onto the passenger seat.

Before starting the car, Ralph brought Sam up to date. "Mr. Crandall called earlier and left a message for Jody. He knew Mom took photos at the ruins, but she didn't recognize three photos were of a young man she knew until the photos were edited and enlarged. Robbie works for Mr. Crandall and has been missing for three days, so he filed a missing person report with Jody because she shops there."

"He looked familiar, but the photo was so blurry."

"He looked familiar to me as well. But like you said, the photo was blurry. Mr. Crandall is headed to the ruins to look for him." Ralph stared out the windshield before adding, "Teddy called just now. Mom's not at the house. He doesn't know where she is."

"I wonder if she went with Mr. Crandall."

Ralph started the car and pulled out of the parking lot. "I wonder that, too. I hope not."

Teddy staggered back to the house and sat for a moment. Taking a deep breath, he collected himself and punched in Ralph's number.

Ralph answered on the first ring and put the phone on speaker. "Teddy? What did you find out?"

"A lot," Teddy said, trying and failing to keep his voice steady. "Mom was at the ruins last night taking photos."

"I know. What else?"

"You know Mom was at the ruins? How did you find out?"

"Just did. Tell me what else you know."

"Where to start," Teddy said, pacing from the kitchen down the hallway to the living room. "I found a chipped piece of brick inside a baggy in the fridge for starters. It has blood on it."

"A chipped piece of brick in the fridge? What do you know about it?"

"I saw a stack of photos on the table beside Mom's chair. I didn't think anything about it at first, then I sat down and looked through them. A car sat in Mrs. Martin's driveway about three o'clock last night. A woman got out and ran around to the back of the house."

"I stopped at the lab to see Sam. She told me about the prowlers last night and showed me the photos," Ralph said.

"Okay. So you know about that. Well, I'll finish because there's something I need to tell you. On the woman's return trip, she fell and cut her hand on one of the bricks that outlines the flowerbed next door. You've seen those bricks."

"Right, I've seen the bricks."

"I saw where the woman sat holding something white against her hand. So, I walked along the bricks until I found one that had been turned upside down. It was dirty and the others were clean. When I examined it, I saw the part Mom chipped off and stuck in the baggy. She even dated it and put it in the fridge. I went next door and Mrs. Martin told me everything. Mom didn't breathe a word of it, because she made Mom promise not to tell anyone about it."

Ralph swallowed as his heart beat against his chest. "What did Mrs. Martin say?"

"Mom and Mrs. Martin drove to the ruins this morning. Mrs. Martin thought it would be therapeutic for Mom because a car followed her from the ruins to the side road you come to. There's no exit. You know the one, right?"

"I know where you mean. It's off Cliff Road."

"Okay. Mom pulled into a dark driveway and hid behind a shed. The person following her drove by then came back. Mom finally left and drove to Mrs. Martin's house. Told her everything that happened." Teddy collected himself before continuing. "They drove out to the ruins early this morning, walked around, then drove up to the top of the cliff. Mom left her to take photos. While she was gone, someone pushed Mrs. Martin over the edge of the cliff and disappeared, not realizing she was hanging onto a root. She would have died if Mom hadn't returned and rescued her! She swore Mom to secrecy."

Ralph exchanged glances with Sam. Her face was as pale as his. "I gather Mrs. Martin doesn't know who did it."

"No idea."

Ralph struggled to maintain equilibrium. "Anything else?"

"Just a few details. After Mom rescued Mrs. Martin and dropped her off, she went into the house. Within twenty or thirty minutes, she left again. That would be to meet Sam for lunch. After that, Mom picked up groceries for her at Crandall's Corner Market and delivered them to her house much later than she thought, so Mom must have done something in between the time she left the café and when she dropped off the groceries. After Mom went home, Mrs. Martin saw her leave about twenty or thirty minutes later."

"Okay, Teddy. Sam and I are headed out to the ruins. Call me if something else comes to mind."

After the call was discontinued, Ralph was silent for a moment as he thought. He asked Sam to punch in the front desk at the police station. "It's Ralph," he said. "Look, I want you to find out where Mr. Crandall lives. He probably lives fairly close to his corner market. I want to know if his car is at his house. Okay?"

In less than five minutes, the phone buzzed. "Yes?" Ralph said. "The neighbor is sure about that? Okay, thanks." His mouth tightened as he stared through the windshield.

"Mr. Crandall's car is in his driveway, right?"

Ralph nodded. "Right."

"That means…." But Sam couldn't finish the sentence.

"That means Mom and Mr. Crandall went to the ruins in her car."

Chapter 40

Jody received the message from the front desk concerning Mr. Crandall. Investigations were typically filled with loose ends and surprises, so this was nothing new. The first parking area next to the ruins was empty, so they drove beyond the ruins to the parking area located on the west side. The only car parked there was identical to the vehicle the Miller family owned. It was a popular make. There were hundreds of them on the road.

Assuming Mr. Crandall had searched the area for Robbie and already left, her mind cast aside the message she'd received and focused on the difficult interviews that awaited her. Yet, in the back of her mind, the thought remained. If he searched the area and left, surely they would have passed a car on Cliff Road returning to Bedford. But they hadn't.

They pulled sufficiently away from the scene to avoid disturbing possible evidence, then made their way across the grassy area for the same reason. They didn't want to contaminate the gravel driveway.

The Miller family sat silently at the picnic table. Beth, a little girl of five, sat on her mother's lap holding her doll, Sally. She had reverted to a long-forgotten habit of sucking her two fingers. Mr. Miller was directly across from his wife and daughter with his two sons on either side of him, his arms around their shoulders. Their heads were lowered, staring vacantly at the top of the table. They were the picture of a close-knit family trying to cope with a shock beyond their ability to handle.

Sitting on the seat pressed against Peter was his dog, Boo. He was a small mixed breed with curly brown hair and an appealing, sensitive face that searched Peter's vacant eyes. Boo went everywhere with Peter except to school.

The second team arrived within minutes, taped off the crime scene, and began standard procedures while Jody and the other officer approached the family.

As soon as Jody spotted the family seated at the picnic table, she recognized them as the people she knew from three years of summer soccer camp. Jody held a short conference with the other officer. The second officer left to join the other team.

It took a moment for the family to realize someone had approached them. Then it took another moment to identify who it was.

"Jody," Mrs. Miller said softly.

"I realize you've suffered a traumatic experience, but I need to talk to Peter—alone."

The parents exchanged glances and nodded.

Peter walked beside the woman who had improved his soccer techniques over the years. Boo followed Peter and sat beside the boy once they were seated at another picnic table, never once taking his eyes off the boy's face.

Jody had interviewed children before. She always started with small talk to give the child a sense that this officer could be trusted. In this case, it wasn't a question of trust, the strategy was to discuss something that gave him comfort then ease into the horror he'd witnessed.

"Peter, I was wondering if you plan to sign up for soccer camp again this summer."

Peter looked up in surprise then glanced away. "Um, probably. I suppose so." He gave it a moment's thought, then added, "Sure. I'll sign up for soccer camp this summer."

"Have you thought about what position you might like to play?"

"Position?" Peter said, his mind touching base with normalcy for the first time since the discovery of the body. "Um, I want to play center midfield. That's an important position. Lots of action."

"You're right. It is an important position," Jody agreed. "Okay. I'll put you at center midfield. It will give you an opportunity to hone those particular skills." She leaned forward, placing her forearms on the picnic table. Peter was beginning to relax just a fraction. Was he ready to relive what happened? Perhaps he needed a few more minutes.

"Tell me how your family got ready for the picnic at your house?"

"Uh, picnic?" Peter said. "Well, we packed the car with all our stuff. Once we were in the car, Dad said let's play a game of I Spy. You know it's the game where you say, 'I Spy With My Own Two Eyes Something That Begins with' and then you name a letter and everybody has to guess what it is."

"Oh, yes," Jody said. "I know that game. So who won most of the games?"

Peter smiled for the first time in an hour. "I did. Then Dad came in second."

Jody smiled in return. "Good," she said then waited for Peter to return to his story.

"So, we got out into the country and Mom always points out stuff for us to look at. Like birds and trees. She loves birds and trees. When we got close to the ruins, Dad saw another car, so he drove past it and parked on the other side and…."

Jody placed her hand on Peter's arm. "You saw another car?"

"Yep. It was parked on the other side of those three old buildings right there," he said, pointing to the large structures.

The ruins blocked the parking area on the east side, but Jody knew there had not been a car when they drove by it. "You're sure about seeing the car parked there, Peter?"

"I'm positive. You can ask the rest of my family. They saw it, too."

"I believe you. Just making sure. Did you see or hear anyone then or at any time since you've been here?"

"No," Peter said decidedly. "For sure, I didn't see or hear anybody since we've been here."

Both were distracted when two officers came into their peripheral vision. They walked slowly along the narrow road on opposite sides, concentrating on the ground. They turned into the second parking lot and made their way up the gravel driveway, careful to keep their feet on the grass so as not to disturb the tire marks. Once they reached the spot where the Millers' car was parked, they knelt and studied the tire treads, then retraced their steps. When they reached the end of the gravel drive-way, they drove stakes into the ground and taped off the last forty feet of the driveway before it reached the road. Having staked off another area, they returned to the other side of the ruins, reexamining the road as they walked.

"What's he doing?" Peter asked.

Jody knew they were looking for tire tracks or evidence that indicated where the victim's killer had arrived, parked, then left.

"Standard procedure," Jody said vaguely, then returned to the question she needed to ask. "You saw a car, Peter. Can you describe it for me?" For the first time, she slipped out a small notebook without looking at it. Her eyes remained on Peter, smiling encouragingly as she opened the notebook and drew out a pencil. "Do you remember anything about it?"

"Uh, well, it was a dark color. Maybe black or maybe dark blue. I'm not sure. It was an old car. I don't know how old, but it looked pretty old."

Again, Jody nodded encouragingly while she jotted down notes and waited. When Peter seemed finished, she said, "Can you remember anything about the car that might set it apart? For example, do you know what I mean by out of state plates? I mean license plates that don't look like the ones you see in Bedford. A different color or design?"

"Oh." Peter's eyes drifted upward. "The license plates where the same colors I'm used to, but that's the only thing I can remember about it."

"Anything else?" Jody allowed the young boy to think. His eyes remained focused upward for a moment, then slowly came down and met her eyes.

"I remember something now."

"What do you remember?"

"There was a dent in the back fender. I remember that because Dad said that car must have been back-ended to get a dent that big. He wondered if the car's brake lights were out. He said sometimes the car behind you will run into you if your brake lights are out and nobody knows you've stopped."

Jody nodded and maintained an outward sense of calm while inwardly she was aware of one car that fit the description perfectly. At that moment, her phone buzzed. It was Ralph. "Excuse me a minute, Peter," she said, then rose and walked rapidly out of earshot. "Ralph?"

"Jody, you're at the ruins, right?

"Yes, I'm interviewing Peter Miller. I know the family quite well. Good people," Jody said. "We're on the west side of the ruins. Karl is here. They're on the east side."

"Okay. Jody, this may seem an odd question, but is my mother's car there?"

Jody hesitated, taken off guard. He may already know something she was about to tell him. "No, but Peter said there was a car parked on the east side of the ruins when they got here. The description he gave of the car fits your mother's car quite well, down to the dent in the rear fender. According to him, they haven't seen or heard anyone since they arrived. I believe him, but I haven't questioned the rest of the family about it."

As anxious as Ralph was to hear the rest of the story, he waited, knowing she was pulling her thoughts together.

"We didn't see Mr. Crandall's car parked anywhere when we arrived. I know what his car looks like. Same thing with your mother's car. It's not here, and we didn't pass a car looking like hers either."

Chapter 41

It was a silent drive to the ruins. Ralph and Sam were occupied with their thoughts. Their eyes automatically searched the parking space located east of the ruins, but it was empty.

Ralph parked his car a short distance from the ruins where the other police vehicles were parked to avoid contaminating areas of evidence as yet unknown to them. Sam collected her bag and camera from the backseat and they hurried to the taped-off area below the pathway.

Karl Farrell saw them coming and met them halfway. "Been dead for several days by the looks of things. At least, that's the initial judgment before the autopsy."

"Several days?" Ralph said, registering the same surprise everyone felt. "Anyone identify the body?"

"Nobody's seen him before. No idea who he is."

"It may be Grayson Matthews," Ralph said. "We need to contact his lawyer to rule out whether or not it's Matthews. Do you know if he's still at the hotel?"

"Called me this morning to check on our progress. Said he planned to stick around till we find him."

"Right. Let's give him a call and bring him up to date. Better give him directions. We don't want him getting lost," Ralph said, gazing over Karl's shoulder at the taped-off area. "Has the body been there all this time and no one's been back here to see him?"

It was a rhetorical question, so Karl just shrugged his shoulders as he glanced at Sam. That was one of the reasons she was here.

Sam left and made her way over the tape to begin the work she came to do. She took photos of the body from several angles, then drew evidence gloves over each hand.

"Look, Karl," Ralph began. "Teddy spoke with my mother's neighbor and there may be a problem. Mom told her neighbor...."

"Myrtle Martin? I know her," Karl said, maintaining a neutral tone of voice.

"Right, well, apparently Mom was here last night taking photos. She thought she was alone. She saw someone along the path, but he disappeared. She took photos of a man on the steps of the ruins. When he started toward her, she felt threatened, and left in a hurry. Apparently, someone followed her at a fairly high rate of speed. Mom couldn't identify the car, although she told Mrs. Martin the car was dark and box-like." Ralph paused to collect his thoughts.

"Could be an SUV."

"Could be," Ralph said.

"Not many people come here this time of year. We'll check for tire marks."

Ralph nodded. "Teddy said Mom turned off Cliff Road onto a side road trying to get away. Have them check that, too," he said. "Mrs. Martin thought it would be therapeutic to return this morning to ease Mom's fears. They came here, parked in the same parking spot, looked around, then drove to the top of the cliff. Someone pushed Mrs. Martin over the edge of the cliff. By some miracle, Mom was able to pull her back over the edge. Has no idea who pushed her."

Karl's eyes were a reflection of Ralph's. "Pushed her over the cliff? Mrs. Martin is just the neighborhood busybody. Who'd want to see her dead? Did Miss Treadwell see who did it?"

"No, Mom was some distance away, taking photos," Ralph said. "Here's where it gets complicated. A young man who works for Crandall's Corner Market went missing three days ago."

"Robbie? I know who you mean. Jody filed a missing person report."

"Right, well apparently three of the photos Mom took last night resemble Robbie. It was dark enough she didn't recognize him when she saw him. And the photos were too dark to identify him on the display panel. Once the exposure was edited and enlargements were made, she called Mr. Crandall and took the photos to the corner market. He agreed the photos resembled Robbie. Where Robbie has been all this time is still unknown. Mr. Crandall called the front desk and explained Mom's photos. Said he was coming out here to look for him."

Karl's brows drew together. "Haven't seen him. And there's no car here except for the Millers' car, and it's parked on the other side of the ruins."

"That's the point. Mr. Crandall's car is in his driveway and Mom's car is missing."

"They drove out here together in Miss Treadwell's car to search for Robbie. And they're both missing. We didn't pass any cars after we got off the main road. Anyway, I know what Miss Treadwell's car looks like and I didn't see it."

Ralph shook his head as he stared at the ground. "Where are they?" he said softly.

"Some of the fellows have been checking tire marks in both parking places and the road in between them. We'll check farther down Cliff Road and let you know."

Ralph lifted his head. "Okay, Karl. I need to talk to Jody."

"She's on the other side of the buildings with Peter Miller."

Ralph walked rapidly to the road, keeping away from any possible evidence that may be contaminated. When he saw Jody and a boy seated at a picnic table, he walked through the grass in their direction.

Jody and Peter both rose when they saw Ralph approach. Boo hopped down, his body alert to defend his boy if necessary. Jody made the introductions, including Boo, and briefed him on the interview, glancing at Peter from time to time to make sure she had understood him correctly. When Peter nodded, she continued.

"Let's talk to the family," Ralph said to Jody, then turned to the boy. "Peter, I'd like you to sit here at the picnic table with Boo for just a few minutes. Okay?"

The two police officers fell into step and observed the other four people they were about to interview.

"Do you want to interview them separately?" she said, which was standard procedure.

Ralph thought as they walked along. "No, let's see how this goes as a family unit."

"Do you want to conduct the interview?"

"You know them well. You do the interview and I'll stand aside."

Jody asked the same questions she had asked Peter, and they corroborated everything the boy had said. She had one last question to ask and expected the same answer. "Did you see or hear anyone then or at any time since you've been here?"

The adults said, "No, we haven't seen anyone since we got here." When they transferred their attention to the younger son, he also shook his head.

But the little girl who leaned against her mother's chest sucking her two fingers while clutching her doll sat up. She took her fingers out of her mouth and said very quietly, "I saw someone."

Chapter 42

Her name was Beth. Beth carried her doll, Sally, everywhere. She took her to the grocery store, to preschool where Sally waited for her in the tiny locker outside the classroom. Beth even took her to the daily summer soccer camp sessions. She sat beside her mother, holding Sally, whispering in her ear while Jody discussed the finer points of playing soccer with the boys, then watched them attempt to follow through on those instructions.

Jody sat with her parents to discuss Peter one day and asked Beth what her doll's name was. When Beth said her doll's name was Sally, Jody said what a nice name that was. She'd had a doll when she was her age and took her everywhere. Beth said Sally went everywhere with her, too. The police officer and Beth smiled at each other and became friends that day.

While her parents and two older brothers carried items from the car to the picnic table, Beth took Sally for a walk. They talked about the wildflowers that had made their way through the thawed ground and now waved gently in the breeze.

Perhaps Beth took Sally just a little farther than she should have. She rounded a corner and saw movement ahead as she gazed through bushes that were too tall to reveal her presence. There was a man carrying a woman and another man walking behind them, sometimes stumbling. Beth watched with curiosity mixed with a certain amount of discomfort. Adults carry children. She'd never seen an adult carry another adult before.

She continued to watch as they rapidly made their way to a car. The man carrying the woman placed her in the backseat along with the man who had trailed behind them. The man carrying the woman drove quietly out of the parking area onto the road.

Beth stood for a moment as she discussed the situation with Sally, then returned to the picnic table. No one asked where she had been. They were busy setting up the picnic and she'd only been out of sight for two minutes. She wasn't a child who needed close monitoring because she wasn't a child who strayed very far from her mother's side. So, she sat and pondered what she'd seen, then slipped her two fingers into her mouth.

Beth's brothers were very talkative, so no one noticed that the little girl was more quiet than usual. Her mother noticed that she ate very little. Her mother felt her forehead and asked if she felt all right. When Beth nodded, her mother continued to observe her little girl throughout the picnic. After her brothers found the body, no one questioned Beth's need to take Sally and sit on her mother's lap. Nor did they question that she reverted to sucking her two fingers. Shock set in. And no one noticed much of anything.

The adults sat in silence as Beth softly recounted her story. Even the two seasoned officers were taken by surprise.

Jody waited until she was certain Beth had finished her story before she said, "Beth, did you recognize any of the three people?"

Beth nodded.

"Tell me about them."

Beth stared at Jody with large dark eyes, then looked up at her mother. "Do you remember the lady at soccer camp who sat beside me one day? She asked me what my doll's name was. And when I asked her if she'd like to hold Sally, she was very excited to hold her. Do you remember that lady?"

Three people sat in shocked silence. Ralph's brows drew together. He wasn't there and had no idea who held Sally at soccer camp that afternoon.

Jody and Mrs. Miller stared at each other, knowing full well who Beth meant. Jody cleared her throat, then said, "Beth, was it Miss Treadwell who held Sally?"

Beth nodded. "Yes, it was Miss Treadwell."

Ralph remained stoic, but everyone felt his deep pain and anxiety by the sudden change of color in his face. He'd been standing. Now, he sat down at the picnic table.

"And Miss Treadwell was the woman being carried?" When Beth nodded again, Jody continued. "Do you think she was hurt or was she unconscious? I mean, did she seem to be sleeping?"

"I know what unconscious means," Beth said. "Her eyes were closed and her head flopped over."

"Did you recognize anyone else?"

Beth thought a moment while everyone waited for her answer. "I know the man who walked behind them. He almost fell a couple of times. He's the man I see at the market Mommy takes me to every week."

"Mr. Crandall," all four adults whispered.

Jody and Ralph exchanged glances. When Ralph nodded, Jody continued. "Beth," she said softly. "Did you recognize the man who carried Miss Treadwell?" When Beth shook her head, she asked another question. "Do you remember anything about him?" When the little girl hesitated, Jody said, "Do you remember what he was wearing? What color his hair was? Was he taller or shorter than Mr. Crandall? Heavier or thinner? Was he older or younger than Mr. Crandall?"

Beth's mind drifted back as she visualized the scene. "He was taller than Mr. Crandall. He wasn't dressed up fancy or anything. He was a little heavier than Mr. Crandall, but not too heavy. His hair was brown and he had a lot more of it than Mr. Crandall, and his face wasn't wrinkled."

Everyone waited until Beth looked up.

"Do you remember what the car looked like?"

Beth sat for a moment as she rocked Sally back and forth. "I think it was the same car Daddy saw when we got here."

Jody turned to Mr. Miller. "I don't remember seeing Miss Treadwell's car at soccer camp. Did you see it?"

"No," Mr. Miller said. "She said she was taking a walk through the park and stopped when she saw Jody. She hadn't realized you were coaching soccer," Mr. Miller said. "That's why we didn't recognize the car when I drove past it."

Jody turned back to Beth. The little girl was very young. Would she understand the next question. "Beth, did Mr. Crandall act unusual or worried or frightened?"

Beth dropped her head. She understood these were serious words. Her memory reached back to the moment she saw the three people walk to the end of the path, then turn and make their way to the car. "The man carrying Miss Treadwell frowned. Mr. Crandall was breathing hard. He leaned against trees a few times when he was on the path. And he almost fell a couple of times. I don't know if he was afraid."

Chapter 43

Every window on the main floor was fitted with iron bars. The front and backdoor were metal rather than wood and were fitted with deadbolt locks, so they required a key to unlock them. Someone had gone to a great deal of trouble to create a prison. But for what reason? The stranger had run into Miss Treadwell and Mr. Crandall by sheer accident. Or had he?

Before climbing the stairs to examine the second floor, they collapsed on opposite ends of the front-room sofa. They rested silently as different possibilities presented themselves.

"He intended for this to happen. And he intended to make us his prisoners," Miss Treadwell said thoughtfully. "But why? You asked him about my purse, but he didn't give it to me when he returned from retrieving it. I know it was intentional. He didn't want me to use my phone to call anyone for help, so he took it with him when he left. And there aren't any phones in the house either. At least none on the first floor."

"Maybe there's a phone upstairs," Mr. Crandall said without conviction. Fatigue was etched in both their voices. "But why would he do that to people he doesn't know and never met?"

"How do we know that?" Miss Treadwell said. "Just because we don't know him doesn't mean he doesn't know us." Then it came to her. It was a slow dawning and she sat completely immobile while her mind drifted back to lunchtime when she looked for a place to park outside Teddy's Café.

"I remember now," she said softly. "I saw that man walk into the police station just before noon today. He was wearing the very same suit he had on when he left here. He wore sunglasses when I last saw him, but he didn't leave here wearing sunglasses, and that can change someone's appearance. My mind was so preoccupied with the photos and meeting Sam that I forgot about him until now."

"Did he see you?"

"No. I'm certain he didn't. His eyes were focused on the front door of the police station."

"What was he doing at the police station? And what was he doing at the ruins? Why did he rent this house? And where is this sister he claims to have?"

"I have no idea what he was doing at the police station. It was a huge risk on his part," Miss Treadwell murmured. "A part. That's it. He's playing two parts, two roles. But what are they?"

"He was in a hurry to get us away from the ruins. When I mentioned we needed to call the police he said the ruins was a dead zone," Mr. Crandall said. He laid his head back against the sofa and closed his eyes. "I'm not sure that's true. I think he just didn't want us to contact the police."

"I agree with you. And I'm convinced he planned this ahead of time. This house has to be part of a larger plan," Miss Treadwell said. "But what is it? Now that we can identify him, will he let us go?"

There was something equally puzzling that had happened in the last hour, and Mr. Crandall struggled to bring it to the forefront of his mind.

Miss Treadwell waited and watched. Finally he turned to her.

"We found the body then left to call the police. We'd only walked a few feet when you fainted on the path. Then suddenly that man appeared and asked to help. He had a nice appearance. Asked me what the trouble was and I said, 'There's a dead body back there.'"

He stopped for a moment and Miss Treadwell said softly, "What happened next?"

"He said, 'A body? A man's dead? Did you recognize him?' But I didn't tell him whether it was a man or a woman. So how did he know it was a man's body?"

Miss Treadwell's mouth went dry. "He knew about the body before you told him," she said. Then another thought arose. "I would expect the police to ask if you recognized the body, but I'm not sure a perfect stranger would ask another stranger if he recognized the body. Perhaps, but I don't think I would have asked that question."

Mr. Crandall shook his head. "I wouldn't have thought to ask it either."

They continued to stare at each other questioningly, then their eyes rose to the ceiling. Someone was walking across the floor just above them.

Chapter 44

Their gaze remained on the ceiling as they heard footsteps walking across the room. The footsteps stopped and the pounding began. "Let me out!" came a muffled, slurred voice.

"Who could it be?" Mr. Crandall whispered.

"I don't know. But there's more than two prisoners in this house," Miss Treadwell said. She rose from the sofa and turned somewhat hesitantly toward the stairway. She was closer and slowly led the way up the steps.

They stopped at the wide landing. Five doors led off the landing. Three doors were open. The bathroom was straight ahead. Two rooms were bedrooms, each containing one bed and one chair.

There was something very disturbing about the bedroom doors. Like the doors downstairs, deadbolt locks had been installed. The occupants couldn't leave unless they had a key. But unlike the doors downstairs, there was a hook beside each door with a key to unlock the doors. Would any of these keys fit the doors downstairs? They doubted it but would try later.

The two older people stood side by side, staring at the door which vibrated with each pounding. Every few seconds the same garbled phrase was repeated: "Let me out!"

It was a man's voice, but it was distorted because of the high-pitched screaming. The key hung on a hook. The stranger had forgotten about this very significant detail. He'd been in a hurry and he'd been careless. The question remained: should they unlock it and free the person? Once the person was free, there was no shoving him back into the room if he proved violent.

"Who are you?" Miss Treadwell said.

The pounding stopped and there was complete silence for thirty seconds. It seemed an eternity at the time.

"Who are you?" The voice was slurred with more than a little suspicion to it.

Again, the older people turned to each other. "Can't hurt to tell him," Mr. Crandall said.

She nodded. After all, the ball was in their court and they didn't have to set him free. "It's Mr. Crandall and Miss Treadwell," she said. "Tell us who you are."

"Mr. Crandall! It's Robbie!" came a tearful reply. "There's someone else locked in the other room. I think he gave her more and she's probably still asleep."

"Robbie!" Mr. Crandall said, his voice rising an octave.

But Miss Treadwell's mind was on a different track. 'I think he gave her more and she's probably asleep'? Who was "her" and what had the man given them? They'd been drugged to keep them quiet. What kind of man would do this? Who were they dealing with?

Mr. Crandall unlocked the door. The younger and older man stood for a moment smiling at each other, then stepped forward and hugged. Robbie was safe.

Mr. Crandall took a firm grip on Robbie's arm as he led him down the stairs one at a time, speaking softly, as a father would soothe a frightened child.

Miss Treadwell took all the keys hanging on the hooks outside each bedroom door and placed them together. They were identical. One key could unlock every bedroom door. But would one of the keys unlock the downstairs door? Quietly, she slipped down the stairs. While Robbie and Mr. Crandall spoke to each other in soft tones, she tried both the front and backdoor but without success. The man had planned this prison very carefully.

Returning upstairs, she stepped through the doorway of Robbie's prison, her eyes sweeping slowly around the room. There was a bed with crumpled sheets, one chair, and a tray on the floor containing what must have been his lunch. At the other end of the room was a door. She opened it and saw what appeared to be a newly installed bathroom with a small sink and toilet right next to it. The walls were the same color as the room. It was obvious the tiny half bath was added very recently, probably just in time to incarcerate Robbie.

Having inspected the little there was to see, she crossed the landing to the other two bedrooms. They were identical to Robbie's room. She stood in front of the second locked room that Robbie indicated was occupied by a woman. Tentatively, she knocked on the door, but no sound came from within.

Curiosity can unlock many unknown doors. Miss Treadwell wasn't sure she wanted to unlock this one. Curiosity may be her undoing nonetheless; she unlocked it and opened it several inches. A young woman lay sleeping on the bed. A luncheon tray rested on the floor. The dishes and drink had been ingested. Evidently, Robbie was correct. They both had been drugged and, while Robbie was groggy, this girl remained asleep.

She crossed the room and stood over the girl. She touched her arm, but there was no waking her. Miss Treadwell's eyes rested on the girl's hair.

One can grow so accustomed to a unique trait someone has that the brain no longer perceives it as unique. That is what happened with Robbie. The customers at Crandall's Corner Market were so accustomed to his hair, they no longer noticed it. This girl shared his unique trait. They must be closely related. His sister?

She had that same two-inch swath of white hair against her natural light brown hair. The white swath ran about three inches deep into her hairline and she brushed it aside. Robbie had the same two-inch white swath in the front of his hair as well. There was no denying these two young people were closely related to each other. They were related, unless….

There was a small door to the left of the bed. It was a half bath identical to the other three bedrooms. She turned to leave, then stood in the doorway. Should she close the door? Would this young woman think it was still locked and that she remained a prisoner? In the end, Miss Treadwell left it ajar several inches, then made her way down the stairs, meditating on the complex details that surrounded these two young people.

They had been made prisoners for a reason. But, without question, she knew Mr. Crandall and herself were prisoners because of these two young people and for no other reason.

Chapter 45

Grayson Matthews' lawyer had been called and given directions to the ruins. Jake Prescott was at the hotel and would leave immediately to determine whether the body was that of his client. Twenty minutes later, a car pulled into the east parking lot beside the ruins and he slowly got out of the car in keeping with someone who may have to identify the body of someone considered not only a client, but a friend.

Officer Karl Farrell recognized the man in the suit with the cufflinks and stuffy kerchief in his breast pocket. On his way to meet the lawyer, he called Ralph. "Lawyer just arrived," he said.

"Be right there," Ralph said, maintaining a neutral voice for someone who had just discovered his mother had been kidnapped earlier that day.

Ralph hadn't met Jake Prescott, but Karl had briefed him with averted eyes and clipped phrases. As he neared the lawyer, he understood Karl's aversion. Haughty and arrogant were the words that came to mind. They didn't see his ilk in Bedford very often.

The lawyer stepped forward, extending his hand. "Jake Prescott. Grayson Matthews' attorney."

"Mr. Prescott," Ralph said, shaking the man's hand while looking directly into his eyes. "Lieutenant Davies, Bedford Police. I know this can be a difficult time and we appreciate your cooperation. If you'll just follow me."

Ralph led the way with Jake Prescott trailing close behind. Ralph didn't use the pathway because the footprints along the pathway were evidence. Sorting through a dozen or so footprints was proving a challenge. They walked up a slight incline, arriving at the taped-off area. He watched the lawyer closely as he viewed the body. There was always sorrow, guilt, regret, or grief, even anger. Often there was a combination of these emotions. What was the prevailing emotion on his face? For the first time in his police career, Ralph saw no emotion. Nothing.

"It's Grayson Matthews. No question about it. Known him for years." Jake Prescott looked up. "Hannah arrived this morning from Cameron. Matthews' daughter. Didn't want to speak to anyone, as you can imagine. Staying at my hotel. I can bring her here to corroborate the identification if you like, but I'd rather not put her through this if at all possible."

"No, that won't be necessary," Ralph said. Jake Prescott continued to stare at the body, which was odd. Most people averted their gaze once the identification was made. But while Prescott studied the body, Ralph studied Jake.

Miss Treadwell kept the sleeping girl's door open a few inches. She looked so vulnerable and so young. Sighing deeply, she turned away and slowly made her way down the stairs, holding tightly to the banister. Steady on her feet, she normally didn't worry about banisters and steps. But the accumulation of shocks and lack of sleep necessitated caution.

Mr. Crandall and Robbie had become quiet, comfortable in each other's presence.

Miss Treadwell approached them and laid her hand on Robbie's shoulder. He slowly looked up. His eyes were still somewhat vacant and unfocused. "Coffee or tea?" she said quietly.

"Tea," he said softly.

She raised an eyebrow to Mr. Crandall. He also preferred tea. The kitchen had been thoroughly examined fifteen minutes earlier, so she knew what was available, otherwise she wouldn't have offered the two men an option of coffee or tea.

It was surprising, almost shocking, how well the kitchen was stocked with supplies for people who were prisoners. But then, the stranger probably stayed here with his sister as well. A thought suddenly crossed her mind. Sister? Was there a woman involved in this, or did he use the security of having a sister as a lure to draw them into the trap?

She boiled the water, brewed the tea, then placed the mugs on a tray along with sugar and milk. Accustomed to a teacup and saucer, she found mugs a bit bulky. But needs must. Surprisingly, there were cookies in the pantry and she placed half a dozen on a plate.

When she returned to the front room carrying the tray, she noticed Mr. Crandall had drawn a small table up to the sofa where they sat.

"Robbie." When he didn't respond, she said his name again, only louder this time. When he looked up, she said, "Do you take milk or sugar with your tea?"

"Just milk."

When she indicated that's how she took her tea, Mr. Crandall busied himself pouring milk into three mugs.

They sat on either side of Robbie, drinking their tea as they observed the young man. He automatically sipped his tea without comment, perhaps forgetting they were even there. By the time he was finished, his eyes seemed a little brighter, perhaps more focused.

This time, when Miss Treadwell called his name, he immediately turned to her. "What happened, Robbie? If you can, start from the beginning."

"The beginning." Robbie looked down at his empty mug, then awoke to a memory. "Miss Treadwell, I understand why you left the ruins last night. I know you didn't recognize me in the dark and you were frightened."

Miss Treadwell closed her eyes for a moment, then opened them and laid her hand on Robbie's arm. "Thank you. I've felt nothing but guilt and remorse since I discovered the photo I took was of you."

"Don't feel guilty." Robbie smiled.

Miss Treadwell squeezed Robbie's arm and was about to ask how he and the girl upstairs managed to reach this house from the ruins, but the young man's mind had moved on.

"The beginning. Uh, I was raised by two people who I thought were my parents," he began haltingly. "When you're young, you don't realize your mother is too old to be your birth mother. By the time I was in my early teens, it finally dawned on me that I was not their biological child." He hesitated again, taking a deep breath, and collecting his thoughts. "They loved me and were so kind to me that I didn't want to bring it up. I didn't want to hurt them. I wanted to be their son. Maybe I was a little afraid of what they might tell me. By the time I was nineteen, they were gone."

"I'm so sorry, Robbie," Miss Treadwell said softly as she remembered the small photo on the inside of the closet door in his upstairs apartment. She took the hand of this vulnerable soul and placed it gently between the two of hers. It remained there until the end of his story.

Mr. Crandall placed his arm around Robbie's shoulders. He had never pried into the young man's past, so this came as a shock to him.

"They left me a little money, but only a little. I got a job, then decided I couldn't live in the house where they'd raised me. I sold it, moved to Bedford, and found Mr. Crandall." His eyes stared vacantly into space as he fought to bring back memories he'd suppressed since their death. "I got a call from a woman who said her name was Vera. She claimed to be a nurse who had been there when my sister was born and my birth mother died."

"You have a sister?" Mr. Crandall said.

"That's what Vera said. She also told me I have a father who's still alive. I had no idea I had a sister or a father. But Vera said I'd recognize her when I saw her."

"Is your sister the young woman sleeping upstairs?" Miss Treadwell said.

Mr. Crandall looked up sharply. He'd been so focused on Robbie nothing else registered.

"I think she's my sister. She has the same distinguishing characteristic that I do. That's what Vera called it: a distinguishing characteristic."

"Do you know anything about her?" Mr. Crandall said.

"She's quiet, so I don't know much about her. She works at a local hotel and lived in Cameron at one time. At least, that's what she said. I noticed her hair was like mine."

"Did she tell you her name?" Miss Treadwell said.

"Hannah. She told me her name was Hannah." Silence followed as Robbie's mind reviewed what he'd said and what he needed to tell them. "A few days later, I got another call from someone who said he was a friend of my biological father. Told me I had a sister, which I already knew. And our biological father wanted to meet us. I didn't particularly want to meet him, but I agreed to it when he said my sister would be there. He said not to forget. I told him I'd never forget but said I'd make a note of it and write it on my calendar when I got home."

Again Robbie's mind drifted for a moment. "The man said he'd pick up both of us at Teddy's Café at six o'clock. I got there a few minutes early and waited, but she never showed up. I left but then a car pulled up. A man got out of the car and told me he was the one who called. He opened the back door and that's when I met the person who is supposed to be my sister." He stared straight ahead as memories took hold then he cast them aside.

"After the call, things began to make sense. You see after my parents died—I still consider them to be my parents—something just wasn't right. I was their only child so there was no one else to go through the accumulation of their things. They'd saved years of bank statements and bills. I never thought about their income. We always had enough. Dad was retired. I don't know. I guess I figured we lived off his retirement."

"You didn't live off your father's retirement income?" Miss Treadwell said.

Robbie shook his head. "I looked through years of bank statements. Every month, a deposit was made into their account. It was the same amount. It was then that I wondered where the money came from. After Vera called," he began, but his voice took on a bitter note, "I guessed where the money came from."

The two older people looked at each other over Robbie's bent head. They guessed where the monthly income came from as well. Even so, Mr. Crandall prompted him. "Do you think the money came from your biological father?"

Tears slid down Robbie's face. But the tears were a mixture of anguish and anger. "After Vera called, I did some checking. That's when I knew who my biological father was."

"Who is he?" Miss Treadwell said.

"Grayson Matthews."

Chapter 46

Ralph experienced the same sensation he had earlier. Something just didn't feel right. "Let's bring in Matthews' daughter. The coroner will want to know why we didn't call in the next of kin," he said to Jake Prescott, knowing full well the coroner wouldn't question his decision.

As an experienced lawyer, Jake Prescott knew that, too. He'd spent decades hiding his emotions in court. That served him well now even though his heart beat erratically. "As you wish," he said. "I'll call and relay the message." Realizing his credibility was on the line, he turned sideways so that only his profile was visible to the officer who was closely observing him. "Hannah, I'm terribly sorry to do this to you, but you'll need to identify your father's body. I realize you just drove up from Cameron and, with the nervous strain, you're tired."

"You're at the ruins?" Hannah said softly into the phone.

"Yes, as I mentioned after I got the call from the officer, I'm at the ruins identifying your father's body, but the police officer feels that it's necessary for you to identify your father as well."

Hannah hesitated, then realized he wouldn't have called if someone could listen in on their conversation. Even so, she kept her voice low. "I really don't want to do this."

"I know it's going to be difficult for you, but I'm afraid it must be done."

"All right," Hannah said in a shaky voice.

"Should I come get you at the hotel, or would you rather be alone on your drive here?" Jake said, using a voice he'd perfected over the years.

"I'll be there in twenty minutes. Is that how much time I should allow?"

"That will be fine. Thank you, Hannah. I'll watch for you." He ended the call, then glanced at Lieutenant Davies. "I'm sure you heard my end of the conversation."

"Yes, it's very difficult but unavoidable," Ralph said. "Obviously she knows which roads to take to the ruins." It was a loaded question presented very casually. Undoubtedly Karl had given Prescott directions, but Prescott had not given them to Matthews' daughter over the phone. The lawyer had thought his identification of the body would be sufficient, so it was doubtful that he had given directions to the daughter. With that thought in mind, how did Prescott suppose the grieving daughter would know how to get to a place some locals had no idea even existed?

For the first time, Jake Prescott hesitated and dropped his eyes. It was ironic because Hannah was exactly five minutes from where they now stood. At the same time, he should have anticipated giving her directions "Well, I'm sure she'll stop and ask."

"Where's she coming from?"

244

"The hotel. I believe I mentioned that."

"Of course. You mentioned that." While the lawyer's eyes remained averted, a half-smile appeared on Ralph's face. A dead man lay at their feet, so it wasn't a smile of pleasure. It was because this haughty, arrogant, big-shot lawyer had slipped up and this small-town cop had caught him at it.

Jake Prescott never displayed discomfort or confusion. He was a man in control of every aspect of his life, and that included his facial expression and body posture. This feeling of being out of control was foreign to him. He did his best not to fidget, but he felt the need to unbutton the top button of his dress shirt, straighten his tie, then fiddle with his solid gold cufflinks. It was a series of erratic fidgeting movements always ending with his cufflinks.

Ralph observed this not with amusement but with growing concern. He recognized fear as well as guilt, although sometimes the two were difficult to distinguish. There was fear with one or two other emotions added to the mix. But what were they?

Hannah paced back and forth inside the Maintenance Building killing time until she needed to leave to identify the body. She needed reassurance. She dug her phone out of her purse. "Aunt Vera?"

Her niece's voice was anxious. "What is it, Sue Ellen?"

"I just got a call. I have to identify Grayson Matthews' body."

Vera closed her eyes. "I'm so sorry. There are so many things I didn't anticipate, and this is one of them. You don't have to go if you feel you can't do it."

Sue Ellen swallowed. "I have to, otherwise—otherwise it's all for nothing. I can do it. I just needed to hear your voice."

Twenty minutes later, a car pulled into the east parking lot. Both men turned and watched a young woman step out. She wore slacks, a shirt, and a jacket. Sunglasses covered nearly half of her face. All tailored and expensive. What stood out was the light patch of hair positioned at the front, trailing several inches back from her hairline.

She stood unsure where to go until Karl led her to the bottom of the slight incline. Her head tilted back, but the dark sunglasses made it impossible to know where her focus lay. She climbed up to the pathway and stood some distance from Jake Prescott. Was she avoiding him or the body that lay at her feet?

"I'm sorry to bring you here, Miss Matthews, but it's necessary to identify the body."

"I understand," Hannah said, her voice unsteady.

Was it nerves or genuine grief? "Would you look at the body and tell me if he is your father, Grayson Matthews?"

Hannah hesitated, then dropped her head. Her eyes lingered on his face, then traveled down his body until they reached his shoes. "Yes, that's Gray—my father," she said, reaching inside a purse for a tissue then touching the corner of her eye.

Did the tissue dampen? From a distance of seven feet, Ralph couldn't tell.

Neither Jake nor Hannah saw Ralph's eyes narrow and a certain firmness settle in around his mouth. Prescott hadn't prepped this girl on how to react. Was she Matthews' daughter but they were estranged so she felt little emotion? Who was she? "Thank you for coming," Ralph said.

"I'll just take Hannah back to the hotel," Jake said. When the police officer didn't object, he took Hannah's arm and they descended the incline together. He opened the car door for her then closed it. Walking rapidly to his own car, he followed Hannah out of the parking area onto Cliff Road.

Ralph joined Karl but was silent.

"How did it go?" Karl said.

"Not sure," Ralph said. "This happened so quickly we haven't had time to verify Jake Prescott's identity. You said he left a business card?"

"Right. It's in my drawer."

"Okay, get the phone number, call his office, and ask for a description of Prescott," Ralph said, then added, "Of course, the business card could be fake and the number you call could be someone he planted to answer the phone and feed you information. But let's start with that. Call the prosecutor's office next. If he's tried cases in court, they'll know him."

Chapter 47

Robbie's revelation stunned the other two into silence. The young man sat still, looking at the floor, giving the other two time to recover.

"Grayson Matthews is the man who came to Bedford County to fish. He's the one reported missing, and he's your father?" Mr. Crandall said, barely above a whisper.

"But how do you know Grayson Matthews is your father?" Miss Treadwell asked. "Were you provided proof that he's your father?"

"The man who picked us up outside Teddy's Café had an envelope with our birth certificates inside. We looked at them, then he took them back," Robbie said. "The fact is I never thought of a birth certificate before. When I was in high school, I wanted to get a summer job, but I needed a social security number. I can remember my parents looking at each other. They said something like, uh, 'You're busy with track and school. We'll take care of it,' or something like that. In a couple of weeks, a social security card came in the mail. They must have contacted Grayson Matthews and told him I needed one."

"I see," Mr. Crandall said, not knowing what other comment to make.

Miss Treadwell dug deeper. "Did you see any similarities between Grayson Matthews and you and Hannah? Was the distinguishing characteristic evident in his hair as it is in yours and your sister's hair?"

Robbie shook his head. "There were two men there. Neither one looked particularly like either of us."

She hesitated because this was going to be very difficult for everyone. "Robbie," she said softly. When he looked up, she continued, "What happened last night? Why were you alone at the ruins?"

Robbie sat for a moment. How could he describe the struggle at the rail resulting in one man's death? How could he explain their frantic search for a place to hide? How could he describe the depth of despair at being caught and brought to this house?

"Begin wherever you like," she said.

"Uh," Robbie began, rubbing his eyes as he struggled to keep his thoughts cohesive. "I got a call at work from somebody who said he was Grayson Matthews' friend—my father's friend. He said there was going to be a meeting and he wanted me to be there. Said my sister would meet me at the café downtown at six o'clock. I was to be there and he'd pick up both of us and take us to where we would meet our father. He said not to forget. I told him I'd write it on a notepad then transfer it to my calendar when I got home."

Miss Treadwell remembered the page torn out of his calendar. Now she knew why.

"I waited for Hannah. When she didn't show up, I left. There was a car parked half a block down the street. A man opened the door and I saw a young woman sitting in the back. I looked at her hair and knew she was Hannah. I got in the backseat. That's when he showed us our birth certificates. He wouldn't let us keep the envelope, so I gave it back to him, then he drove out of town into the country. I don't have a car or any friends besides Mr. Crandall and my landlady, Helen. I'd never been that far out of town before. Hannah hadn't either. We were both scared."

"Did he take you to the ruins?"

"We drove past the ruins and up to the top of a cliff. He parked the car and we followed him at some distance. Someone else was there, but we didn't notice him until the man in front of us stopped."

That was an odd turn of phrase, and she questioned Robbie. "'The man in front of us stopped'? I thought the lawyer drove you to the top of the cliff. But you just referred to him as 'the man in front of us'."

Before he could respond, they heard footsteps on the stairs. Hannah had awakened and was slowly making her way to the first floor. Robbie rose and met Hannah at the bottom of the steps. She looked over his shoulder and saw two strangers.

When Hannah stumbled, Robbie placed his arm around her shoulders and led her slowly to the sofa. The older people moved to the sides, giving them space to sit in the center.

"Hannah, this is Miss Treadwell and Mr. Crandall." It seemed odd making formal introductions at a time like this. But they were making an attempt to follow social conventions even though they were all prisoners and their future was uncertain and possibly very brief.

Hannah's eyes were glazed over, as Robbie's had been a short time ago. Turning her head was beyond the scope of her ability, but she attempted a smile.

Miss Treadwell studied the girl, then asked the same question she had asked Robbie. "Tea or coffee, Hannah?"

Hannah sat next to Miss Treadwell and slowly turned her head. "Coffee, please."

Miss Treadwell carried the tray back to the kitchen. Once the coffee was brewed and cookies were on the plate, she returned to the front room. All three of them observed the awakening as Hannah's eyes slowly came into focus. She also had a story they wanted to hear.

"My aunt raised me. She gave me my name. I knew my mother was dead, and my aunt never spoke of my father although I asked her about him many times. She said she'd tell me when the time was right. But the time never seemed to be right."

Hannah sipped her coffee, placed her empty mug on the tray, glanced at her watch, and resumed her story. "It was several months ago that my aunt revealed certain facts about my parents. Nothing much. My mother's hair was the same as mine." She turned to Robbie. "And yours, too."

Robbie's eyes misted. This was the first time he'd heard anything about his mother. "I'm glad. I'd rather look like her."

"Me too," Hannah said softly. "About two months ago, my aunt went into a room she used as an office and shut the door. I heard her making phone calls. That happened frequently over the next few weeks. Somehow, I knew it had to do with my parents. One day she came out of her office and I knew she was going to tell me things I might not like. She told me my mother died the day I was born and that, because of her death, my father was a very wealthy man. She told me other things about our mother's death. I became angry and decided to leave Cameron. I knew it hurt her, but I just needed time to process everything. I moved to Bedford because she told me my brother lived here. I knew he called himself Job, but I didn't know his real name or his address."

Miss Treadwell compared the two young people. Robbie still seemed a bit dazed from the after-effects of the drug he'd been given. But Hannah appeared quite alert. Had she been given less of the drug? Or perhaps she hadn't been given the drug at all.

She observed the young woman as she spoke. Twice, she'd checked her watch. Was it out of sheer habit or was there a timetable that must be adhered to? When Robbie recounted the events, he did so haltingly and rather reluctantly. He was drawing from a repressed memory. But Hannah's speech was very fluid. There was no stumbling and no pauses. It was almost like a speech she'd memorized, a part she'd rehearsed for a play in the theater. As the uneasiness grew, so did the suspicion. Who was this young woman?

Chapter 48

Hannah gazed out the side window during the trip from the ruins to the hotel.

Prescott grasped her arm as they walked through the hotel door. "Keep your head down and let me do the talking," he murmured. "I can't have anyone you used to work with recognize you and start asking questions."

It was the dinner hour, so the hotel's restaurant was conveniently crowded. There was a table for two in the corner and they sat there with Hannah's back to the room. She didn't see anyone she used to work with but she didn't want to take any chances either.

Jake Prescott ordered for both of them while Hannah buried her face in the menu. When the server left, he sat back and surveyed the room. "Everything is going to plan more or less."

"More or less," Hannah replied.

They ate in silence. Prescott ate his food while Hannah toyed with hers.

"How long till Mathews' will is probated?" she said.

"Probably a year. But I've moved all the liquid assets out of the country. There's only a small amount of the estate left. It's enough to cover the funeral expenses and probating the will."

Hannah placed her elbows on the table and leaned forward. "How could you do that? You don't have the authority to move Grayson Matthews' assets out of the country."

Prescott lifted an eyebrow. "Power of Attorney."

"You have Power of Attorney over Matthews' assets?"

"That's right," Prescott said.

"How did you manage that?"

"My dear girl," Prescott said in a patronizing tone. "I'm his lawyer—was his lawyer. He signed whatever I placed in front of him."

Hannah dropped her eyes. When she felt more in control, she said, "What about his two children? Don't they have a right to a share in his estate?"

"Sure," Prescott said offhandedly.

"How is that possible if most of the money is out of the country?"

"There'll be a few thousand left after expenses are paid."

"I see," Hannah said, for she understood completely what his intent was. "Do you think that's fair?"

Prescott sighed deeply. "Look, I made a deal with Gray's daughter. She's helping me with a few things and she'll get a larger piece of the pie. Okay?"

Hannah sat back speechless while Prescott continued to consume his food. She wasn't aware that Jake had made a deal with the woman posing as her. "How did you manage that?"

"I needed someone on the inside. When I spoke with the son, I knew instantly he was unapproachable. The daughter jumped at the chance. That is how I managed it."

Hannah understood why Aunt Vera wanted her in this position. The imposter who represented her was to get a chunk of the estate while the two legitimate children got nothing. "What about the four people at the house?"

"What about them?"

"When do we let them go?"

Prescott leaned back in his chair, wondering if he'd made a mistake in hiring her for this job. "We don't."

"They have food for maybe two weeks or so, then they just starve to death? Is that it?"

"No, I've made arrangements for someone to, uh, see to that," he said vaguely.

"For how long?"

"Till I'm out of the country," Prescott said, then decided this might be a good time to part company. "Give me your key to the house." He gazed out the window and said casually, "I left my key at the house when I changed clothes."

Hannah gave a convincing performance of searching her purse. "I must have dropped it somewhere."

"I see." Two could play this game, Prescott decided. "You need to find it today or you don't get paid."

Hannah decided to leverage the information she'd withheld. "I've discovered something."

"What do you mean?"

"The taller woman you saw on the cliff?"

"Okay, the taller woman," Prescott said. "What about her?"

"Her name is Cynthia Treadwell. The car is hers as well as the camera."

"Yes, well, she resides in the house now, so we really don't have to worry about her." There was a look of triumph in Hannah's eyes. "Just tell me what you know about her."

"Cynthia Treadwell's son is Lieutenant Ralph Davies of the Bedford Police Department."

Prescott's fork was partway to his mouth. It froze for a moment, then he slowly lowered it to the plate. "She can identify me," he murmured.

"She could identify you before you knew who she was."

"Yes, but this will be personal with Davies."

"If he finds his mother unharmed, he may be more gracious toward you," Hannah said.

"Only if he finds out." Prescott punched in a number on his phone and waited, then pressed redial and waited again. He stared at his watch. "It might be too late."

"Too late for what?" Hannah waited anxiously. "Too late for what?"

"I have to leave. You stay here."

Before Hannah could object, Prescott walked rapidly out of the restaurant. Seconds later, she saw him trot to his car and pull out of the hotel. Leaving her dinner unfinished, she rose and walked to a quiet corner in the lobby. With trembling hands she retrieved her phone from her purse and made a call. "Aunt Vera, I identified Grayson Matthews' body forty-five minutes ago."

"Are you all right?"

"It was horrible! It was the first time I saw my father, and he's dead," Sue Ellen said, then gathered herself. "Prescott just left the hotel."

"He left the hotel? Why?"

"The woman posing as me is working for Jake. I don't know what she's capable of doing, but she's in the house with Robbie," Sue Ellen agonized. "Miss Treadwell and Mr. Crandall are there as well."

There was silence on the other end as Vera absorbed more frightening pieces of unexpected information. "What else?"

"I told him who Lieutenant Davies' mother is. That was a mistake. I shouldn't have told him," Sue Ellen said. "I told him if Lieutenant Davies finds his mother unharmed, he may be more gracious to him. Then he said, 'Only if he finds out.' He tried to call someone twice but there was no answer. I suspect he was trying to call that girl. Then he said, 'It might be too late.'"

"Too late?" Vera said. "What might be too late?"

"He didn't say."

"Do you know where he's going?"

"Not for sure," Sue Ellen said. "But I think he's headed to the house."

"Okay, I'm quite a bit closer to the house."

"Do you have the key I dropped through your mail slot?" Sue Ellen said.

"I have it."

"There may be an easier way. The police are at the ruins and Lieutenant Davies is with them."

"Okay, that's where I'm headed," Vera said. "Sue Ellen?"

"Yes, I'm still here."

"You need to stay where you are until I call you. Will you do that?"

Sue Ellen struggled to obey her aunt. "I'll stay."

Chapter 49

The front desk at the police station had been very busy that afternoon. When the phone rang again, the officer on duty answered it using his standard voice. "Bedford Police Station."

"This is Hattie Freemont. I am a law-abiding citizen!" the woman began.

"Yes, ma'am," the officer said, trying to keep the tiredness out of his voice.

"Now, we bought this house ten years ago because it is off the beaten path and that's just the way we like it."

This line of dialogue would go on forever if the officer didn't alter its course. "Yes, ma'am. Can you tell me what the problem is?"

"Well! We go days without a car going past our house. In the past two weeks—well, might be longer than that if you count the trucks. At least the trucks were respectful of the speed limit. Now, in the past few nights this car has raced back and forth in front of our house I don't know how many times! Last night it was two cars. Squealing tires and all kinds of noise!"

"Have the trucks or cars trespassed on your property?"

"Well, no! But the speed limit going past our house is forty-five. These cars must be driving at least sixty, maybe sixty-five. Squealing tires and…."

"There's been more than one car?"

"Not until last night. Some folks moved in around the bend a week or two ago. There's been plumbing trucks and carpentry trucks and I don't know what all driving by here."

"Sounds like they did some remodeling before they moved in," the police officer said as another officer smiled and shook her head.

"Yes, well I need an officer to park a car nearby to catch him the next time he goes tearing by our house."

"I see. Where do you live?"

"You know Cliff Road? It's off the main road leading to the ruins."

The officer sat up. "Cliff Road? You live off Cliff Road?"

The other officer stopped what she was doing as she heard Cliff Road repeated.

"Right, Cliff Road. It's a narrow road. Our house is about a half a mile from the main road."

"What's your address?" the officer said firmly. When she gave it to him, he said, "We'll be there in ten minutes." As soon as that call was disconnected, he called Ralph. "Ralph, I just got a call from a Hattie Freemont who lives off Cliff Road. This is what she reported: 'In the past few nights this car has raced back and forth in front of our house I don't know how many times. Last night it was two cars. Squealing tires and all kinds of noise.'"

Ralph's head lifted and met Karl's eyes. "Off Cliff Road?"

"Right, off Cliff Road. She said it's a very quiet neighborhood but everything changed in the last two weeks. Plumbing and carpentry trucks drove by, then people must have moved in. Those are the ones with 'squealing tires.'"

"Okay, thanks," Ralph said. "Give me the address and we'll take it from here." He briefed Karl, then said, "This may be nothing more than an exasperated neighbor. But nobody saw Mom's car on the way here and it may be because it pulled off that side road. I want to keep a low profile with this. We'll take my car." As they walked to Ralph's car, he gave Jody a quick call. "Hattie Freemont filed a complaint. Cars exceeding the speed limit in her neighborhood. She lives off Cliff Road. Karl and I are responding to it. I need you to cover the east parking lot."

"On my way, Ralph," Jody said.

Ralph's voice and manner were calm, but once behind the wheel of his car, they arrived at the house within minutes of the officer's call.

Hattie Freemont opened the door before Karl had an opportunity to knock. "You the police?"

Karl was in uniform, so it seemed an odd question.

"Yes, we're from the Bedford Police," Ralph said.

"You in charge?"

"I'm Lieutenant Davies. This is Officer Farrell."

"Aw right," Hattie said. "Better come in." She stepped aside, then led them through the living room where her husband was watching a football game with the volume set at a deafening level. "Can't hear a thing with that TV on!" she shouted. "Best go into the kitchen."

Once the door was closed and the three were settled at the kitchen table, Hattie didn't wait for questions: she unburdened her frustrations to a willing audience. "I need my peace and quiet," she began.

The seasoned police officers kept a neutral face in spite of the temptation to roll their eyes.

"Started a couple of weeks ago, I think. All kinds of trucks whizzing by here. Then all kinds of cars doing the same thing. We spent good money buying this place and…."

"Can you describe the cars, and did you notice how many people were in the cars?" Ralph said.

"Not too good at cars," Hattie said. "One was darkish and squarish. You know, those modern things that block your view when they're parked next to you at the grocery store and you can't see to back out."

"Right, I know what you mean," Ralph said. "Like an SUV?"

"Whatever. Couldn't see too much of the inside because its windows were darkish. Hidin' from the law I suppose. Now, earlier this car I never seen before comes whizzing by and…."

"Can you describe it, and did you see the occupants of that car?" Ralph said.

"Just happened to be at my window," Hattie began. "Like I said, not too good at cars, but this was one of them older cars, darkish, bluish I think. Had a dent in the back fender. Let's see. People," Hattie murmured. "Well, the driver looked younger than the two older people in the backseat." Hattie stared at the ceiling. "That's all I can tell you about it. Wasn't even an hour later that a different car came whizzing by the other way heading towards Cliff Road. That same SUV I was telling you about earlier. Then, not too long after that another car I never seen before drove past, but she minded the speed limit."

"She," Ralph said. "The driver of the second car was a woman?"

"Youngish woman."

"Can you describe the car?"

"Well, it was just a regular car," Hattie said. "Sorta tannish, newish, had four doors, could see the inside, which is why I knew it was a youngish woman."

Ralph and Karl knew which cars Jake Prescott and Hannah Matthews drove to the ruins to identify the body. Mrs. Freemont had just described them.

Prescott claimed he and Hannah had driven from their hotel to the ruins. This woman just destroyed that claim.

Chapter 50

Jody heard a car approaching at a relatively high rate of speed. Everyone else heard it, stopped working, and waited. A middle-aged woman got out of the car. Jody recognized her. She didn't know her name but she'd seen her at the corner market. Saw her leave the market, cross the street, and enter a rowhouse.

Just then, Sam walked rapidly to her side. "Jody, where's Ralph?"

"He and Karl left to talk to a woman who lives off Cliff Road," Jody said. "What's happened?"

"I've examined the area carefully," Sam began. The woman was nearly upon them, so she finished her sentence quickly. "The body of Grayson Matthews was moved. I'm not sure where it originated, but it's been moved."

"The body's been moved? Okay, I'll tell Ralph. Thanks, Sam." Sam returned to the pathway and Jody turned to meet the woman.

She walked with her shoulders back and her head held high. She was fairly tall with brown hair and eyes. She wore a dark pant suit with a white tailored shirt underneath. She stopped directly in front of Jody and said, "Do you recognize me?"

"I've seen you at Crandall's Corner Market several times, but I don't know who you are."

Without identifying herself, the woman said, "I live across the street from the market. Helen, Robbie's landlady, and I have become friends," she said. Making connections to people others know is always helpful.

Jody nodded but didn't smile. "Yes, I know Helen and Robbie. What can I do for you?"

Time was of the essence. Once she'd gained a certain amount of trust, she got to the point. "Cynthia Treadwell and Mr. Crandall have been kidnapped and I know where they are being held."

"Who are you?" Jody said quietly.

"I'm sorry, Jody. I'd prefer to reveal my identity to Lieutenant Davies."

This woman knew her name as well as Ralph's name. "Very well, I'll take you to Lieutenant Davies." She and the unknown woman sat quietly in the back of an unmarked car while an officer drove them to Hattie Freemont's house.

Once there, Jody quickly made her way to the front door and knocked. When Mr. Freemont answered the door, she said, "I need to speak to Lieutenant Davies immediately."

Mr. Freemont was a man of few words. He opened the door wider and pointed to the kitchen door.

Both officers rose quickly and followed Jody outside, where the woman stood waiting beside the car. Jody quietly briefed the men on the way.

Ralph moved forward and, without any formalities, said, "What can you tell me?"

"I know where your mother and Mr. Crandall are."

"Where are they?"

"The house is around the bend about half a mile from where we're standing. It's the only house along that strip of road."

"How do you know that?"

"I've been there, Lieutenant."

"Who are you?"

"My name is Vera Matthews. I'm Grayson Matthews' sister. And I know Jake Prescott," she said. "I've lived across the street from Crandall's Corner Market for three weeks."

Jody nodded when Ralph glanced at her.

"Are Miss Treadwell and Mr. Crandall the only two people in the house?"

"No, Robbie Matthews is in the house, and there's a young woman called Hannah who appears to be working for Jake. I know this because I've been in constant contact with someone connected to Jake."

"Hannah," Ralph said. "Does she work at the hotel?"

"It's a rather confusing story, Lieutenant. My niece, Sue Ellen Matthews is posing as Hannah. She worked at the hotel. The woman at the house with Robbie is posing as Robbie's sister and Grayson Matthews' daughter."

It was confusing but Ralph needed answers. It was more important to gain access to the house without anyone getting hurt. "Have you been in the house?"

"Once, but there were no occupants then. There are four bedrooms

269

and a bathroom upstairs. Jake converted all the bedrooms into prison cells with a half bath in each one and deadbolt locks for the bedroom doors. It appears Jake wasn't sure how many people he would need to imprison. The downstairs dining room is currently used as a bedroom."

"That's an expensive conversion."

"There's a great deal of money at stake, Lieutenant."

"You seem to know Jake Prescott fairly well."

Vera dropped her head, then looked up. "Grayson, Jake, and I grew up together. Jake lived two houses away. We walked to school together. We know each other very well."

"Do you realize your brother is dead?" Ralph said more gently.

"Yes, I know Gray is dead. We've been estranged for years. Even so, he was my brother."

Ralph saw a certain amount of controlled grief in the woman's eyes. Time allotted for grieving would have to come later. "What can you tell me about Hannah?"

"Very little, I'm afraid. I can't tell you whether or not she's armed or dangerous," Vera said. "One more thing. Jake Prescott is on his way to the house this very minute. It would be safer for those four people if he didn't see us standing here." She checked her watch. "I've been here exactly four minutes, so there's not much time left until he arrives. I know where we can park the cars out of sight until he passes by."

"We'll follow you," Ralph said.

Two cars backed out of the driveway with Ralph following the car holding Vera Matthews. They drove a short distance and pulled into a long driveway with a shed at the end. The house looked deserted. The lead car pulled around the shed with Ralph directly behind it. The shed was wide enough that the cars were invisible to anyone on the road.

They positioned their cars facing the road. Ralph apprised an officer at the ruins of the situation and told him to be ready to move out with the next call. Not knowing what they faced, Ralph presented a strategy asking Vera if she'd be willing to be a part of the team. When she agreed, they situated themselves on either side of the shed. Moments later, Jake Prescott's car raced past.

Jake broke every speed record he'd set in the years he'd been driving. He pressed the redial button countless times, furious that she wasn't answering even though he'd instructed her to silence her phone. He knew it was too late, yet he held out hope that there'd been a delay and there may still be time to salvage the situation.

Chapter 51

The three sat waiting for Hannah to continue her story, but her story appeared to have drawn to a close. She glanced at her watch. "I could use another cup of coffee," she said. "I'll make another pot of tea while I'm in the kitchen." When Mr. Crandall rose to help, she waved him back on the sofa. "I can manage."

While they waited, Mr. Crandall and Robbie spoke quietly. But Miss Treadwell's focus was leveled at the sounds coming from the kitchen. For a prisoner locked in her room, she seemed quite familiar with the kitchen. Instead of opening and closing cabinets and drawers multiple times searching for items, only one cabinet and drawer were opened and the refrigerator. Within minutes, Hannah returned carrying a tray with four mugs, a pot of tea, and a small pitcher of milk. She poured milk into three mugs then filled them with tea and handed them to each person. Picking up her own mug of coffee, she leaned back and began to sip.

How did Hannah know they drank milk with their tea? Miss Treadwell pondered that thought, drew the mug to her lips and stopped.

There were tiny particles floating on the surface. So tiny had she not been peering through her bifocal lenses, she would have missed them. She glanced to the side. Neither Mr. Crandall nor Robbie appeared to have noticed.

Hannah prattled on about her time in Bedford in between sips of coffee and rotating glances of the three people and her watch.

Miss Treadwell drew the mug to her lips, tipped it, then allowed her left hand to hover over the top of the mug, suggesting she was a bit chilly and this helped to keep her warm.

How to warn the others of her shaky suspicion escaped her. Perhaps the miniscule floating material was milk that had started to curdle. She'd feel like a supreme alarmist if that was the case. But if she was correct, she was condemning two innocent people to whatever fate was contained in the tea.

Robbie's eyes were losing their focus, looking much the same as they'd appeared forty minutes ago. He moistened his lips, then said, "What's your real name?"

"My real name? Hannah is my real name."

Robbie blinked slowly. "Your real name? But when Vera—I mean when Aunt Vera called me, she said you only called yourself...."

Mr. Crandall's head fell back on the sofa and his mug slid to the floor. Seconds later, Robbie followed suit.

Miss Treadwell knew Hannah was waiting for her third victim to collapse. The cloth sofa would absorb liquid. She couldn't allow her mug to fall to the floor because Hannah would realize none of it had been consumed. Pressing her mug against the lower arm of the sofa, she tilted it and allowed the liquid to spill between the arm and the cushion.

When enough had been deposited, her mug fell to the floor with what little remained and her head sank back. As her head rested on the sofa she pondered Robbie's question. What's your real name?

Hannah shook all three victims. When there was no response, she rushed up the stairs to her bedroom. With no one to listen in on her conversation, she didn't shut the door. She dug her phone out of its hiding place. Numerous calls had been attempted in the last fifteen minutes.

"Jake? I had the phone turned off. They're all asleep. How soon can you get here?" Hannah said. "What do you mean 'oh, no'? That was part of the plan!"

"Look, don't do another thing till I get there!" Jake said.

"This was supposed to be just Robbie if you recall. That was the deal. Now there are two other people involved."

"I know. Can't be helped. But there's a complication."

"What kind of complication?" Hannah said guardedly.

"The woman, Cynthia Treadwell. Lieutenant Davies is her son."

"So, he finds the body of his mother and two other people instead of just Robbie."

"Bodies!" Jake said. "There aren't supposed to be any bodies."

Angered by what he said, Hannah chose to ignore his question. "When do I get my share of the estate? I want to get out of here as soon as this is over."

"What do you mean your share of the estate? I never promised you a share."

"I'm supposed to be Grayson Matthews' daughter. I'm entitled to a share. You get half the estate and I get the other half."

"Look, I, uh, we'll settle everything tonight when we reach Cameron." Silence hung heavily for a moment.

"How soon will you get here?"

"Two minutes. Making the turn off Cliff Road right now."

Hannah stumbled down the steps and unlocked the front door.

Miss Treadwell's heart raced as she watched through slitted eyes. Hannah had the key to the front and back door hidden. What to do? Was it safer to feign unconsciousness? A car approached and pulled into the gravel driveway, skidding to a halt. A door slammed shut and suddenly the man who had kidnapped them appeared. She closed her eyes completely.

"We can't just leave them here and walk away," Hannah said. "It's not that they know too much. They don't know anything. But when the police question them, they'll be able to piece together what happened."

Jake stood halfway between the open doorway and the sofa. "I know, I know. Let me think."

"Look, what are three more bodies? There's already one on the pathway below the cliff!"

"That was different! It was Diablo or me," he said. "And you know that. You were there."

"Maybe I know that and maybe I don't."

Jake studied the young woman. "You'd turn against me?"

"Not if I get half the estate."

The two were so focused on each other, they failed to hear someone walk through the door.

"Hello, Leto."

Chapter 52

Jake whirled around. "Vera. How—what are you doing here?"

"My brother was killed," Vera said. "I'm sure you're aware of that."

"Vera, it's not what you think."

"That's comforting, Jake. You and Gray always had a contentious relationship. I'm relieved to know it isn't what I think."

Jake glanced at Hannah, whose expression was a combination of shock, fear, and fury. "Could we have this discussion later? I'm, uh, rather busy just now. Why don't you go home or wherever you're staying and I'll meet you later."

"We can't let her leave," Hannah said.

"I'll handle this!" Jake said.

"Like you handled Gray?" Vera said.

"Vera, it isn't what you think," Jake repeated. "Hannah was there. Tell her it was an accident."

But when eyes turned to Hannah, she hesitated. "Well, I'm not so sure it was an accident, Jake."

Silence hung in the room.

Miss Treadwell's half-opened eyes traveled back and forth as accusations were made and defenses proclaimed. Jake and Vera were directly in front, but Hannah stood at a forty-five-degree angle two feet from her so that only her right side was visible. Helpless to do anything, her only defense was to remain still and wait.

"What do you mean?" Jake said in a raised voice.

"Just what I said. I don't remember what happened. Not exactly. Could be you just picked up Grayson Matthews and tossed him over the side."

"Don't be ridiculous!" Jake shouted. "That's impossible! We were equally matched. It was a struggle from beginning to end."

"End is the right word," Hannah said. Where the gun came from, no one knew. She looked pointedly at Robbie. "He's first!"

"He's your brother!" Jake shouted.

"He's not my brother!"

Jake froze. The shock gave Hannah just enough time to raise the gun.

Miss Treadwell leaned forward and grabbed Hannah's arm. A bullet was fired. She slid off the sofa and crumpled to the floor.

Four officers converged in that room. Jody and Karl entered from the kitchen, Ralph and another officer through the front door.

Jody called the emergency number while she hurried to the kitchen to collect anything that would staunch the bleeding.

Ralph knelt beside his mother. Her shoulder was bleeding. "Tell the ambulance we'll meet them at the end of Cliff Road."

Karl and the other officer took charge of Jake Prescott and Hannah.

Ralph carefully carried his mother to the first police car and climbed into the back seat next to her. Jody slid in on the opposite side pressing a clean towel to Miss Treadwell's wound.

Robbie and Mr. Crandall were helped to the car and taken to the hospital in the second police car.

Within minutes, they met the ambulance at the main road, the transfer was complete, and they followed it to the hospital.

Jody had called Teddy. He was already there waiting.

As in the fall of 1995, Ralph, Teddy, and Sam took turns watching over Miss Treadwell in the hospital three rooms down the hall from where she'd previously stayed. For three days, they sat holding her hand, whispering soothing words to her. She was sedated to ease the pain and keep her shoulder still, but she was aware of her hand being held, and soft, comforting voices. From time to time, her eyes opened partially and a thin smile creased her lips.

On the fourth day, she opened her eyes. Teddy's chair was next to her, his hand held hers, and his head rested on her bed. "You need to go home and sleep, Teddy," she said softly.

Teddy lifted his head. "You're awake."

"Yes, I'm awake. How long have I been here?"

"This is your fourth day," Teddy said. "How are you feeling?"

"A bit sluggish. Shoulder hurts a bit. What happened?"

Teddy hesitated. "There's someone in the waiting room who can start from the beginning if you're up to it."

"I want to know what happened."

Chapter 53

Teddy left the room and returned with a woman who took Teddy's place.

"My name is Vera Matthews," she said. "I'm Grayson Matthews' sister."

Miss Treadwell studied the woman's face and saw intelligence, character, and deep sadness. A memory returned. "You're the woman at the corner market."

"Yes." Vera smiled.

"Helen?"

"Yes, I've become friends with Helen. She took great care of my nephew, Robbie."

"Your nephew," Miss Treadwell said. "I'd like to hear the story if you're willing to tell me."

"Growing up, the four of us went everywhere together. My brother, Grayson, Jake, Anne, and I were inseparable. The boys detested the nicknames they gave each other. Gray was Diablo; Jake was Leto.

"Anne was a shy, sweet, sensitive girl. She was just part of our group until Gray discovered she had a trust fund. Gray made her feel special, important. He married her trust fund. But he grew tired of being the husband of a wealthy wife who controlled the purse strings. Gray wanted out but had become accustomed to the lifestyle Anne's money provided."

Vera stopped for a moment, judging whether she was exhausting Miss Treadwell's reserves.

Ever perceptive, Miss Treadwell said, "I'm all right. Please go on, Vera."

Vera continued. "Robbie was born. His sister followed two years later. Anne's second pregnancy and delivery were normal. At some point after she was transferred to a regular room, she began to hemorrhage. Gray was alone with her. When I walked into Anne's room there was blood everywhere. Gray stared at me. We both knew what happened and what he failed to do."

Tears threatened and Vera paused as she collected herself. "I'm sorry," she whispered. Her hand lay on the bed and Miss Treadwell placed her hand on top of it.

"I'm a nurse. Even though I knew it was too late, I called for help. When the stat team arrived, Gray suddenly became the grieving widower.

"I stumbled to the waiting room and called Jake. First he was shocked, then he was furious. He spoke of justice. Diablo murdered his wife for her money. I listened and let him rant. We agreed we would always remember Anne.

282

"The entire estate went to the two children but Gray was their father and would oversee it until they were of age. He enjoyed the wealth. More importantly, he controlled the money and didn't want to share it with his children who were entitled to it. He sent me monthly checks for Sue Ellen which I saved. I raised Sue Ellen. I didn't know where Robbie was."

"Your brother didn't tell you? How painful."

Vera nodded. "It was. Gray placed him with an older couple some distance away and they gave him their last name. It took years to find him. I talked to the older couple. They loved him and I didn't want to upset his life. When Robbie reached twenty-one, I called him. I knew what needed to be done would set off a chain reaction. I just hoped I could contain the fallout," she said, looking at Miss Treadwell.

"You couldn't have anticipated everything that happened."

"No, I didn't anticipate most of it. I feel as though so much of this is my fault."

Miss Treadwell squeezed her hand. "What happened was inevitable no matter who initiated it. You did it for them."

"You're right. I did it for them," Vera said then continued her story. "After I spoke with Gray, he called Jake. By the time Jake called me, he was very angry. He said he'd heard from Gray only because Diablo was worried about losing the money to his children. Jake contacted a private investigator we'd known since we were kids. He pulled together an elaborate plan where Robbie, Sue Ellen, and Gray would all meet and discuss the situation at a remote area."

Vera paused again. During that pause, Miss Treadwell perceived a deeper issue. "But you were worried."

Vera nodded. "I was worried what Jake might do. Normally, he was a level-headed lawyer. But Anne had been allowed to die and his fury had been brewing for years.

"I spoke with the private investigator at length and we decided to switch roles with the two girls. Jake lived in New York and never returned to Cameron, so he didn't know Sue Ellen. Hannah had worked for Jake before but the two had never met.

The private investigator hired Hannah to play the part of Robbie's sister while Sue Ellen played the part of Hannah. She wore a beret to cover her hair. Sue Ellen had referred to herself as Hannah for some time, so the transition to being called Hannah was an easy one for her to make. That way, Sue Ellen could report to me daily. Sue Ellen got a job at the hotel under the name Hannah Bennett and waited for the plan to begin." She paused and dropped her head.

"But there was a death you could not have foreseen. And in no conceivable way can you hold yourself accountable for what others did," Miss Treadwell said. Her voice was weak but her words were firm.

Word came that the jury would return shortly with a verdict, and Miss Treadwell wanted to be present. She walked slowly, but unaided, into the courtroom and sat with Teddy, Mr. Crandall, and Myrtle Martin. Seated in front of them where Ralph and Sam. On the opposite side of the aisle, Vera sat between Sue Ellen and Robbie Matthews with Helen sitting next to Robbie nervously holding his hand.

The jury returned and the judge asked whether they had reached a unanimous decision. They had and the foreman of the jury stood. "We find the defendant guilty."

The courtroom was silent except for the judge who thanked and dismissed the jury. Everyone rose with the judge, who left the courtroom.

A broken Jake Prescott appeared calm and resigned yet anxious as he searched the room for his childhood friend. When he found her, his eyes sought forgiveness. He silently mouthed the words, "I'm sorry."

Tears rose to the eyes of Vera Matthews. Their gaze held but a second. When Vera nodded and gave a rueful smile, Leto turned and followed the policeman through the door.

~The End~